Topsy Turvy
my life in the year 2013

A novel by Anne Wilensky
Cartoons by Bill Pyne (aka Billy
Stampone)

Published by Haiku Helen Press

Published April 2014
© 2014 by Anne Pyne

Written, edited, and published by Anne Pyne
Cartoons inside book by Bill Pyne aka Billy Stampone

Cover drawings (front and back) by Helen Kritzler.
Cover designed by Helen Kritzler

ISBN 978-0984097685

Contact information: Willard Kraft
(520) 465-0999
5152 East 8th Street, Tucson, AZ 85711

First edition
Printed in the United States of America.

Thank you

Muchas gracias to everyone in Tucson for being so swell to me. I am grateful to have all you angels in my life...

And for my great angels who help me so much. Frank Grijalva and Bill Kraft. Better friends a girl could not have.

And for the great angel Manuel Andrade. Who saved my truck for me on Chanukah and made me so very happy.

And thank you too to the girls in my little email group. How could I have made it thru that long dark cold strange winter of 2013 without having you girls to confide my life to each morning when I woke up

All of you together, boys and girls alike, have been my life in this year 2013. I thank you all from the bottom of my heart.

Love Annie

The day before Christmas 2012

Yesterday I went back to my driving

Jim doesn't have an easy time putting up with Anne

Yesterday I went back to my driving. I haven't driven since the rains came. I no longer remember when that was. It feels like a world ago.

I hadn't driven in so long that when Jim suggested it yesterday I knew if I didn't do it now I would never do it again.

I had lost all connection to driving. The last two times I had done it had not been a good experience.

It had been far too tense for me driving in town. Driving in traffic with other cars on the road. It had not been pleasurable at all. I hadn't wanted to do it again.

It just seemed so much simpler to let Jim drive me everywhere, sit back and relax.

Yesterday was cold but bright sun was shining. It was Sunday. I really did feel like *now or never*.

"OK" I said. "Let's go to the country then. You can wash the windshield for me when we stop on the way for gas."

I was quiet all the way. I have no grip on my mood at all now. I have no idea what makes me want to laugh and play and kid around with him in the car. Like the day before when he had driven me for my errands.

Or why I was so quiet yesterday. Why I just wanted to sit quietly and say nothing. Look out the window. Just be quiet.

We stopped for gas, he washed the windshield. I went inside and bought two peanut butter on crackers.

He drove me to Corona Road. Without any fanfare at all

we changed seats and I simply began driving.

I drove slowly the whole time. He went out of his mind the whole time. All the way up Corona Road, all the way down Los Reales, all the way to the end of Swan Road, I drove slowly. I had it in 4th but never went above 20 miles an hour.

He went out of his mind the whole time. He insisted every which way to Sunday that I step on it.

I was the only car on the road the whole time. I figured I wasn't bothering anyone.

He carried on that I was going 20 miles an hour. "I put up with it when you do this in your own neighborhood," he kept saying. "I don't want to put up with it now," he kept saying.

"Tough" I said. "Turn on the radio" I said, "you can listen to the radio."

The truck has no radio. This is a joke I make to amuse myself.

"The speed limit here is 55 you have to go the speed limit," he said.

"You can read the article about the Mass Awakening by Archangel Raphael while I'm driving.

"You can read it aloud to me" I said.

"I won't read it," he said. "Archangel Raphael is a nut."

"Turn on the radio then and listen to the game."

"There is no radio" he said.

"Now you are going 15 miles an hour!" he said.

"You're lucky you're going for a nice drive in the country on Sunday morning. Not every friend would do that for you. You are lucky to have a wonderful friend like me."

No man was more miserable as he was driven that long forever stretch of Swan Road with not another car on the road by me at 20 miles an hour.

"This is torture," he kept saying.

I didn't care. I knew the best thing for me in whole world now was to be relaxed behind the wheel again. There had been a long time of me driving where I hadn't been relaxed at all. And it had taken its toll. I hadn't wanted to get behind the wheel again as a result.

I didn't mind all his complaining. It amused me. It gave conversation in the car while I was driving. It diverted me.

"Awww the open road" I said with enthusiasm.

"This is not the open road!" he said, "the open road is not driving 15 miles an hour."

I chuckled to myself.

"I love the open road" I said.

When we reached the end of Swan Road I did 6 tushy turns right in a row. That is what Jim and I call the 3 point turn which I have to do successfully on the Road Test to get my license.

They got to be called tushy turns because Jim kept saying "you turn the wheel in the direction you want your tushy to go," meaning the back of the truck.

Oddly enuf it relaxed Jim when I did 6 of them all in a row, and all of them perfectly. He had really wondered if my driving had regressed in long month of not doing it.

He thought maybe I really had gone back to square one. But I was so relaxed at driving such a long distance at only 20 miles an hour, it made me relaxed while I was doing my tushy turns. So I was able to do them fine.

I am beginning to see the whole key for driving for me is being relaxed behind the wheel.

On the way back to Los Reales Road I drove the same way but this time Jim did not complain. He was overjoyed by my tushy turns.

"I am not seeing any animals," I said.

"There aren't any animals," he said.

"I wonder why?" I said. "There aren't any birds in the

sky," I said looking up at the huge sky.

I said "We may as well get my cartons of cigarettes at the rez while we are all the way out here.

"You give me the directions till we get to Nogales Highway then we will change seats."

"You can drive on Nogales Highway" he said.

I ignored him.

I followed his directions till we came to a long stretch of road I hadn't been on before. There were cars on it but not that many. It was Sunday. It was fun for me to be on a road I had never been on before. With different view on the sides and a different view ahead of me.

By now I was relaxed and warmed up. I drove like a normal driver. I don't know why, it just seemed to come naturally to me. It felt natural going at a faster speed. Cars passed me who wanted to go faster. Fine with me. But I knew I was going a natural speed now. And it was fine.

Then I pulled expertly into the embankment right before Nogales Highway and let Jim take the wheel.

After we bought a whole box of cartons of cigarettes. And after Jim stopped at Nico's along the way home so I could get take-out Mexican food to eat when I got home, we got to my driveway.

"I'm not going to swim today," I said. "You did enuf. You helped me a lot. Just bring the cigarettes into the house for me then you are a free man all day."

Before we reached my house, a few miles up, he said "you drove spectacular."

I couldn't believe my ears. "Say it again," I said. "Say it again."

He said "Not in the beginning. In the beginning you were a black hole You got an F. But at the end you drove spectacular."

"Really?" I said. "Really? Say it again" I said.

After he brought the box of cartons of cigs into my bedroom closet he noticed my cat Priscilla curled up in her chair. He stopped to pet her and give her love.

She loved all her pets and love and attention. The girl was in bliss. It was very nice for me. Bill is an animal lover. He always gave our dogs and kitties too so much love and pets and attention.

There hasn't been a man in my house giving Priscilla love and pets and attention since Bill is no longer here. It made me remember how much I love men, how sweet they are, how loving they are.

With both Bill and Jim you never get to experience their

loving sweet side until you see them with an animal. That is when they express their whole loving side. And it is always bliss for me to stand back and watch it.

The pet is in bliss and I get to see the man who is my closest friend turn into a being of such total love you can just stand there and swoon. It is like a little bit of Heaven taking up residence in your house.

You get to watch pure love happen right in front of your eyes.

It's very very special and I love it so.

I love being in the country even when I drive slower than the cyclists..

LOL I guess this sweet driving lesson was the last day of my old life. I woke up Christmas morning to all my electronics plotzing.

First my email stopped working. Then my computer blew up. My phone wouldn't work and my TV went to Heaven.

As soon as I got all this squared away in early January, I plotzed too. An unbelievable fatigue swept over me while I sat at the computer. I staggered into my bed and could not get up.

The transition had begun in earnest.

Cold dark winter

I knew I was going somewhere, but where I had no idea

Months later I tried to describe my strange winter to my friend Jimmy Goldiner back in NYC.

Hi Jimmy

2013 has been the strangest year in my whole life so far. And I am sure it will continue to be.

My outer life has not changed one whit, or barely at all, but my inner life sure has gone thru huge changes. Giggle giggle it's almost as if on January 1st my inner life set off on a bizarre voyage.

LOL I guess like a voyage to the bottom of the sea. I went all the way to the bottom of my memories and emotions for night and day for almost 6 weeks.

I did not eat or sleep. I just lied under the covers on the cot in Bill's tool room next to the furnace (the house was freezing cold, Tucson was having sub freezing weather).

This is not something I chose to do, it all happened to me. Suddenly out of nowhere on January first a fatigue hit me, that was all powerful.

I remember I was at my desk at computer when it

happened. I staggered to the tool room which is room next to my computer room, got under the covers.

And that *thing* began. Just all intense memories from the past.

The fatigue was so great I could not even leave the tool room except to make the monumental effort to get up to go to the bathroom.

Yet I never slept. Occasionally I would doze for a moment or two and when I did my dreams were just as intense and on the same topics as my waking thoughts.

They were not at all like normal dreams and did not take me away at all from my night and day experience in the tool room. Also the moment or two of dozing off did not relax me or refresh me. It's almost as if the purpose of it was just to send me those dreams.

Which were almost like post scripts or commentary on my dark intense waking thoughts. They did not illuminate what was going on for me. It was just a way to add to my thoughts in a different way.

What made it hard is I didn't know what was going on or why it was happening. But I was with my Higher Self all thru it. So I had the security of knowing that for whatever reason this is what was meant to be happening in my life now.

Altho I had instantly plummeted down to the bottom of my mind the same instant that fatigue hit me. Rising up from the bottom of my mind and from that extraordinary fatigue was a slow process.

I spent 3 weeks night and day at the place at the bottom of my mind. Altho at some point I would force myself to get up to let Jim take me swimming and then return to the tool room cot instant I got home for another day and night of it.

And at some point I even drove around my neighborhood with Jim a little before swimming.

That is when I got pulled over by the cops and had that shocking experience.

But the shock changed everything.

The experience with the cops was so huge for me. It propelled me upwards from the bottom of the sea in my mind. I began the long slow climb back up to the surface of my life.

I still wasn't eating or sleeping. It was still night and day sessions with my deepest and most disturbing memories from my past. But I did get up each day to spend an hour at my computer emailing.

I wanted to be in communication with the world again. Because I had been on a group email with some of the girls who had been in my women's lib group back in the '60s in NYC, we all got on email together a few months before this *thing* happened.

We had stopped talking about women's liberation and were now just confiding our day-to-day lives to each other. I felt so close to them.

I never explained to them what was going on. I didn't understand it myself, so how could they! But I did email them almost every day during my day-to-day climb back into the world.

Love, Annie

Here are Anne's emails to her little group

Being stopped by the cops is no fun

I still do not have my drivers license, I have not yet taken my second road test. I had a big bump in the road 3 days ago because a girl cop pulled me over for driving in the bike lane.

I know that it is a no-no, but I was trying to go to the mini post office in my neighborhood. And when I wanted to make the left turn to it, I saw so many cars bearing down behind me, I just pulled into the bike lane so I would be out of everyone's way while I decided what to do.

Turned out there was cop car behind me and she had me pull into a driveway.

I had to sit there a whole hour. She discovered my learners permit had expired. Two times I got out of the truck to go over to her to find out what the problem is. I was starting to feel like I had committed a major crime.

She ordered me back in my vehicle. When I tried to ask her a question, she said "Do you have a comprehension problem?"

I said "no."

She said, "You were told to stay in your vehicle."

Then she said "Have you been drinking this morning?"

I said "I am insulted, I have never had a drink in my life but I want a cigarette."

She said "Get back in your vehicle!"

Jim my friend who is teaching me to drive was scared because they took his license too and he thought they would give him tickets for everything I did because he is my licensed driver.

Also they said they were deciding if my truck had to be towed home.

Which makes no sense, Jim is there and can drive it home.

Finally the man cop came out to give me the two tickets. For driving in the bike lane and for expired license.

He asked me how long I have been learning how to drive, and was kind and understanding. She had been so hard assed with me and said "You are not allowed to drive barefoot."

I still don't know why it took her a whole hour, she must have been looking up all my violations.

It really shook me up and it shook Jim up too.

Love Annie

P.S. Ruthie looked it up on internet. It is *not* against the law to drive barefoot. I go to court on February 28th.

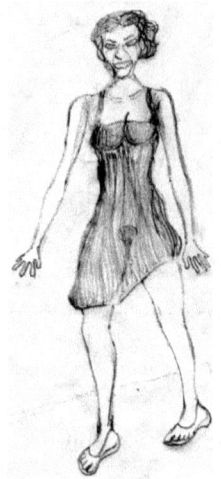

Anne is ordered back into her vehicle two times

Jim took me swimming after the cops drove off

LOL Anne is stunned from her experience

But the next day I went down to DMV to get a new learners permit

Sent: 8:43 AM
Subject: I flunked the written test yesterday, today I take it again

I flunked the written test when I tried to take it yesterday morning.

Today I will have Jim take me back. I read the Drivers

Manual all day yesterday and maybe that will improve how I do today.

But it is a tricky test, and if it means I flunk again today and have to go back tomorrow. So what!!

I will just keep going back till I do pass it.

And maybe it's not such a bad thing that my new life is going every morning to take the written test at DMV.

Love Annie

Anne accepts her new life is taking written test every morning

Later that day I email them again

Good news I passed the written test this morning

The test is tricky and difficult. Altho I think easier for an experienced driver who already applies all those things all the time.

Half the time I had to guess, very few answers did I know the right answer.

You are allowed 6 wrong out of 30 questions. If you get a 7th one wrong, you flunk.

Because of the computer they tell you how many wrong answers you already have and how many more questions there still are.

When I saw I already had 6 wrong answers and still had to answer 23 questions I got very nervous.

After that each time I guessed, before I chose my guess, I said to myself "if it is wrong I'm not going to cry."

It was such a miracle to me that I actually passed.

And it was still early enuf for me to have my swim afterwards which was a huge treat.

I wish you all a great evening.

Love, Annie

My misadventures began on Christmas morning

Patty is my sweet friend from Fort Lowell Public Pool

Hi Patty

I did get your loving Christmas email but my computer crashed the next day and I was not able to write back to you.

It took 3 weeks for my computer to be fixed, finally it is back from central repair and I am back on it.

Also at the same time my television went to heaven. I had to go to Target and buy a new TV. I did not know how to program it.

My friend Jim was technician for the gas company here in Tucson, but knows nothing about computers and did not know how to program my new TV either.

I became desperate when everything broke at once, because I was used to having Bill who did everything for me.

I called up my kid brother in San Francisco in tears and said "you have to come out here and help me."

He knows how to do that stuff. He did not want to come out here but offered to pay the money for me to hire someone.

So I said "Send me $200 to give to Jim because it means so many times he has to unplug everything and take it to Office Depot and then pick it up and plug it all back in."

Jim did not know how to do it and was scared.

But Jim wound up having to do it 5 times, because the first time Office Depot said "It will cost $350 to fix your computer and you have to wait 3 weeks. But we will sell you a brand new one for $400. Just pay $50 to transfer your hard drive."

So I thought that was a good idea. But after Jim managed to plug it all back in for me, the new computer turned out to be defective.

So we had to bring it back. Manny gave me another new one and transferred my hard drive again, and when this turned out to be defective after Jim got it all plugged in again.

Manny (the wonderful man at Office Depot) said "Just

return it, and we will send your computer out to be fixed."

When it came back from central repair Jim managed to plug it all back in again with my printer and my scanner.

But he inadvertently did something to the printer. So then he had to unplug the printer and take it to Office Depot so they could get rid of the paper jam.

Finally by a miracle now everything is working again.

Meanwhile the techie from COX had to come 3 times to get my new TV programmed.

Can you believe all of that since Christmas morning when I first woke up and discovered I could not email.

And now that that is all taken care of, this week was the drama with the cop. And yesterday I was at DMV taking the written test for the second day in a row.

But I passed the test. I have another valid Learners Permit and I am on email with you and receiving all your tender love.

Please give Mike all my love and thank him for helping you email me.

Love Annie

I had fun at the doctor

I haven't been to the doctor in 20 years. The last time I went was when I first moved to Tucson. I had an allergic reaction to the pollen. The doctor gave me an inhaler. I went to the doctor yesterday to get new one.

From: Annie
To: Jean and Peggy and Ruthie and Pat and Heather and Casey and Jo
Sent: Friday, January 25, 2013
Subject: I had so much fun going to the doctor yesterday

I had a lot of fun going to the doctor yesterday. It was a huge adventure for me. First Kelli interviewed me and I confided about my abortion when I was 20 years old and also about smoking pot all thru my twenties.

She was way too young to know how dramatic it was to get an abortion when it was illegal.

But I had fun dropping my voice dramatically and leaning forward confidentially when I told her.

Same thing with smoking pot. Who now does not!

But still it was so much fun being dramatic about it. Telling her all about it in a secret voice and very close up.

Giggle giggle I had a ball.

She took my blood pressure and tried to take my temperature. I got so excited, I said "I have not had my temperature taken since I was a little girl, my mother was a nurse."

However it was electronic, she could not succeed. Finally I said "Why don't you do it the old fashioned way and put your hand on my forehead to see if it is warm."

She explained "We don't use that system because of subjectivity. The observer changes the outcome."

Isn't that the Planck uncertainty principle.

The behavior of the atom is affected by the observer.

Kelli is the first one in the whole world to use this principle to explain why putting her hand on my brow won't give accurate temperature.

So you get an idea of the wonderful time I had at the doctor yesterday.

Then Kelli went out and Doctor Connie came in and Connie went up and down my back listening. I guess about 6 times. I found it very enjoyable.

Love Annie

Email February 8ᵗʰ

Back in circulation

The wind has been blowing all day, a small wind, but still strong and persistent. There is determination there.

I am grateful today was not being stopped by the cops, not having to go down to DMV and take the written test again.

When Jim called to take me swimming he suggested we do some driving first.

I thought it was a great idea. I was afraid I had taken against driving after my recent bad experiences, so I was curious how I would feel behind the wheel again.

I said "OK but just in my own neighborhood."

It did feel good and it did all come back to me. And it was nice to be relaxed behind the wheel and enjoying it. And kibitzing with Jim as I drove.

It took a while for my happiness to come back, it may be

a while before I feel so merry and light again, I had such a big encounter with the State.

I woke up thinking it is time for me to email my friends again. Other than emailing with our little group I had not emailed a soul since my troubles began on Christmas morning.

Today I decided to get back in circulation. I emailed my big cousin, my little brother, and my friends from the public swim pools, and told them about my cop adventure and taking the written test again.

And I emailed Bill's sister in San Diego too.

Even if everyone is too busy to respond to my emails now, it still feels good to be back in circulation again. It makes me feel like I have my life back, which I haven't since Christmas and all the changes happened.

I did kid around a lot with Nancy in the swim pool and lifeguard John this morning, and it is the first time since Christmas that I was relaxed enuf to want to kid around again. So maybe I am lightening up.

Love Annie

Email February 13

The return of my energy...

Today was a very nice day. Perhaps it is the return of the energy. For the first time in weeks it was on the qui vive again. Life felt normal, it felt alive, the bubble of enthusiasm was back.

Everything was enjoyable. My swim was enjoyable. Shopping in the supermarket was enjoyable. Being with Jim was enjoyable. He was in a good mood too, a very good mood.

He was the one behind me in line in the supermarket so I didn't have to worry about being a pain in the neck to the person behind me. I could take as long as I wanted. And even ask the check-out guy how to get cash after I paid for my groceries with my credit card.

Of course Jim teased me all the way home that the reason it took him so long was because he was behind a meshuginar on line in supermarket. (Meshuginar is crazy person in Yiddish). He learned that word from me and now it is his favorite word.

After he teased me about being behind a meshuginar on line, he teased me about my comprehension problem.

"The cashier didn't understand about your comprehension problem."

I am never going to live it down that Officer Jeffries asked me with all seriousness "Do you have a comprehension problem?"

But it was fun for the shoe to be on the other foot for a change. Usually I pick on Jim from morning to night, I find it so much fun to tease him.

He has put up with that for 2 years, he is allowed to get his own back.

And it was nice for me to be laughing all the way to swim pool and all the way home from supermarket.

Also he imitates how I drive which for some reason I find very funny.

If Jim's great mood is a sign that things have changed, spirits have picked up, I am all for it.

All I can guess is past 6 weeks were physical, mental, emotional renovation.

Hahaha maybe now the era of happiness has begun.

Another thing which was different is I had an idea again. I had an idea for a project I would like to work on with a friend of mine.

Even if the friend doesn't want to do the project when I tell him, I realize I was inspired.

And I can't remember the last time I was inspired.

That seems like another very good sign too.

Love Annie

February 14th

Life is coming back

It is a beautiful morning in Tucson. Altho **c-o-l-d**. There is frost on everything in the yard. And I am in front of my open window in 2 skirts, a sweater, and a sweatshirt.

But on the desert when the sky is cloudless, it warms up as the sun rises higher in the sky. It is just a little after 8 am now, by noon it may be warm enuf to lounge in sunshine in a sundress.

My spirits have gone back up and my energy has come back in, and that is the main thing. I feel like a different person, or at least that I am having a different life.

Even tho I am not doing one thing differently (my days are the same) there has been a sea change in my thoughts. Like the trees in my backyard which are now reaching upward because the sap has risen, my thoughts are reaching upwards too.

They were mired down for 6 weeks and there was not

one thing I could do about it. It's as if they were under some kind of pressure which kept them tight and intense.

There was simply no such thing as them taking off, becoming airborne, going anywhere. It was like 6 weeks of being in my own mind with no escape.

Altho sometimes that got interesting too. I felt like I was starting to know myself or know my own mind. I thought "Is this what it was like for those yogis in ancient India who would go off to a cave for a year?"

Maybe that is what I felt like. It was too cold to be outside, I was trapped under the covers with my thoughts.

But one thing which did come from it was the breaking up of all my mental habits. I was able to see my life differently.

Sometimes it would go from extremes. One afternoon I remember it started out with me in tears "What a terrible life I have! I have nothing in my life at all!"

But the thoughts continued and continued and by the end of that "session" I came to the opposite conclusion. I just saw it all differently.

"My life is perfect" I saw, "everything about it is perfect, it suits me perfectly."

And in a way when this period is over, I don't know if it

is over, maybe just the darkness and intensity is over, there is more brightness now, there is more light and there is more life. My thoughts have finally switched over to activities I want to do, projects I want to start.

Life is coming back.

My sense of humor is returning...

I did have an odd evening last night when I was alone with my thoughts. On one hand I thought "I can't go on like this just chit chatting with my Higher Self, I want people in my life I want to have fun."

My Higher Self said "I'm fun."

"No you're not," I said "you're not fun."

"I am too fun," She said.

"You're no fun at all" I said.

"I am lots of fun," She said.

Somehow it made me giggle arguing with My Higher Self about whether She is fun or not. Me insisting She is no fun at all, and Her insisting She is so much fun.

The argument made me giggle.

And after that I noticed my sense of humor has come

back for the first time in 6 weeks. It is the first time I laughed at my life again or laughed at myself.

It seemed before my life hit bottom or whatever it did for past 6 weeks— went thru a tunnel, had a transformation— before that when I had regular life, I did have a sense of humor about my life. I wasn't always so dead serious.

My thoughts were not this intense.

But after My Higher Self insisted She is a lot of fun to hang out with, I will admit my sense of humor came back.

First I thought about my teenage boyfriend Lewis who had called me few days ago late at night and promised he would call me back.

He hasn't called me back yet but I keep looking forward to the phone call. Even if it never happens I notice it is fun to look forward to a phone call.

He had called me because I had mailed him a few of my books and he had actually started to read my little womens lib book. He called because he had read first 2 or 3 chapters and wanted to tell me he really liked it.

He has a jazz program on the public radio station in a small town in California. Jazz was always his whole life even when we were young teenagers together. And I think it is made to order for him that they let him have his own jazz show on the public radio station there.

Before I sent him my books I told him one was on women's liberation. That was the one he was interested in. He said he had interviewed an author on his show about women's liberation.

So when he called me few nights ago and said he's reading my womens lib book and really liked it, he said "You used one word I didn't know what it meant. All your words are so simple but this word I didn't know what it meant. Wait I will find it!"

He looked for it and said "The word is apotheosis, what does that mean?"

I said "I don't know, the top?"

He said "Do you think you misused it?"

I was floored. I never heard of anyone asking an author if they think they misused a word. For some reason it made me laugh for 5 minutes.

He said "Maybe we better look it up, maybe you misused it."

"Sure" I said "look it up."

But when he read the dictionary definition to me, I swooned. Its meaning is so beautiful and it means what I said about that womens liberation meeting that night was so beautiful.

And when he read me the next two sentences on the phone, I said "That is really touching." I hadn't realized I said anything touching about womens liberation.

I was happy with myself.

Then he said "I see you always write *altho* instead of *although*. Why do you do that?"

I said "I don't know, I did it since I started writing."

"O I see," he said "it's an affectation."

And for some reason that made me giggle too. LOL it is another insult.

But then the next day I called him and said "You know it could be a nice jazz program. You read a little of my writing and then put some jazz with it."

He said "I'm walking out the door I'll call you tonight about it."

But he never called back and I don't know if he will.

But yesterday evening when I was wondering if he will call back about it I thought, "I wonder if he will do another segment for his show of "Insult The Author."

It just seemed so funny that the way he had "interviewed" me for my little womens lib book was by insulting me.

Of course it wasn't a real interview, but I still thought "If he does call back I will tease him about his *Insult the Author* segment."

And that made me laugh.

Well it is bright sunshine outside. I have no idea what I will do today.

But maybe I will schlep my comforter out into the sunshine

I wish you all a wonderful Sunday.

Love and kisses Annie

Email February 18 7 PM

The adventure of the Mustang's dent

The sun is going down but the unusual light which came in this afternoon is still here.

It makes the world look uncanny. You walk outside to put a bill in the mailbox and you feel like you have walked into a fairy tale. It is so unusual and lovely.

Today was a nice day, altho unusual too. A few years ago Bill and I bought a second hand Mustang, it is also a clutch. So when Jim was driving me everywhere, in exchange for that favor I loaned him our Mustang.

This is a huge favor to him since it meant he lent his old car to his niece. And he no longer has to spend every day, all day, driving her places.

Because she has two babies, his whole life had been driving her places. Now she can drive herself in his old car, and he zips around town in my Mustang.

It's a perfect plan, because the Mustang had to be driven anyway, and when he drives me somewhere I get to choose whether to go in my truck or my Mustang which is a convertible.

Yesterday Jim's friend called him up and said "My son's car won't start will you drive him to work."

Jim said "of course."

But after he dropped the young man off at Racquet Club where he works, Jim got call on his cell phone. He wasn't paying attention and backed into a dumpster, which took out the rear light and made big dent.

My Higher Self said "It's not fair Jim be punished when he is doing a favor for a friend. So you should offer to pay half of everything, for the new light and for getting the dent fixed."

Jim asked Frank to call his brother in law. Frank's brother in law (Manuel) is the one who took out all the dents in my truck. I had really banged it up during my driving lessons.

And Manuel did a beautiful job and is so reasonable. He works in his backyard.

Of course things work their own way when you call Frank and say call your brother in law and then wait for

Frank to call back.

It was 24 hours of no one calling anyone back. And wondering how it will work.

But it is now 24 hours later. Frank says his brother in law can do the job on Wednesday, he will pick up the Mustang from my driveway. Jim just has to drive it over the day before. I will lend Jim my truck so he has wheels.

And Frank is going to find a place in Tucson which sells the rear light, since it is smashed.

I will stay home all day Wednesday in case Manuel actually does come to pick up the Mustang that day.

I actually think having 24 hours of dent drama has been good for me.

I was so deep in my inner life that it was good to be pulled out of it. To be on phone with Jim about the dent, and talk to Frank about it when he took down some branches in my backyard this afternoon.

Maybe because I'm not the one who did the dent, and am just being swell to Jim by helping him. Whatever it is I think the experience is just what the doctor ordered right now.

It has pushed me back into the world and I wanted to be back in the world.

Last night I giggled to myself and said "It is *The Adventure of the Mustang's Dent* and it is time for a new adventure in my life."

Love and kisses, Annie

February 18th

Emails to a New Age friend

I do have one friend who is just as New Age as I am. Back in NYC in the late 1970s we were writers together. Writers just starting out.

When she and her husband moved to Tucson 13 years ago, I found out she is no longer writing. She discovered water colors and she prefers that.

But to my amazement and joy I discovered she had become just as New Age as I am.

All my beliefs had changed, it was nice for me to have someone to share it.

LOL it made life easier for my husband too. Each time I would try to talk New Age to him, he would interrupt me. "Tell your friend Jan," he would say, "she believes the same things you do."

And I would.

We'd talk on the phone once a month and email regularly. It was a big joy in my life.

Like me she had believed heart and soul that the Winter Solstice 2012 Mass Awakening would actually happen.

Together we had looked forward to it for years.

The evening before it was supposed to happen I called her. "I guess if it doesn't happen we will get a consolation prize."

She said "we will get a booby prize" and I laughed for ten minutes.

Well it didn't happen, at least not the way it was billed, and instead she spent the same winter I did.

We both began our re-entry into normal life at the same time. And would email to compare notes about it.

Here are my emails to her today

Email at dawn

Hi Jan

I actually slept last night.

Sleeping thru the night is still a new thing for me. It didn't start to happen till last week and it means I wake up so relaxed in the morning.

I think I knew this "thing" was really over when I began to sleep thru the night.

Dawn is starting now. It means a slight indigo light is coming in from the East and the Full Moon is still shining in my West window.

First bird chirped in its nest.

I woke up optimistic about life which is a nice way to wake up.

I really can't remember when I last had that feeling. It may be a few years.

It sure feels nice to wake up relaxed and happy and optimistic about life. Even if it doesn't last.

Ever since 2013 began my life bounces from one extreme to the other just like our weather has been doing.

But maybe this time of transformation (the past 8 weeks) is ending. Hahaha we are now transformed. And it means we can start to have happy days again too.

An hour later

The beautiful morning has just started

It is so much fun seeing the big pigeons all arrive

Sitting on my telephone wire

I love it when the birds arrive in my backyard

It is so much fun watching them

O the sun must have risen above mountains because sunlight is now splashing into my view out west window

O the color and the beauty

We are so lucky to live in this paradise.

I wish you and Harry a lovely day.

Love Annie

Later the same day 5 pm

Hi Jan

This afternoon I got discouraged. Then I read the *Letter From God* for today which I had printed up this morning. It overjoyed me when I read it this morning.

I had it in my backyard to read it again. After I realized I was discouraged I did read it again.

All about the amazing absolutely wonderful experience that will happen to all of us.

So then I thought "I may as well believe it. The girl who let herself be tricked into believing the Mass Awakening would actually happen may as well let herself be tricked into believing this amazingly wonderful experience will inevitably happen to all of us."

LOL I never used to be sarcastic about all this spiritual stuff but as my Higher Self pointed out the other day "It was a letdown for you that the Mass Awakening did not happen."

Love Annie

February 22

Fun with Dr Connie...

I woke up to another cloudy overcast day and turned the heat back on.

I am thinking of just staying home today and not going anywhere. I had far too much excitement in my life yesterday than I am used to.

It began with Jim driving me to Dr Connie. The pharmacist said the doctor won't refill the prescription. And when I called, the receptionist said "the doctor has to see you to refill it."

So I arrived at 9 am yesterday and had to wait practically 2 hours. First a very long time in waiting room. Then a long time in the examining room too.

It seemed senseless that I had to wait two hours and be examined again just for a refill when I had just done all this last month to get the original prescription.

I was patient all thru it, till almost the end.

Then I thought "If I have to do this again I'll ask Jim to drive me to Mexico. The pharmacy is right on the other side of the border in Nogales. And Nogales is just an hour from Tucson.

"They sell the same inhalers there and you don't need prescription for it. Actually they have a 3 pack.

"By the time it takes for Doctor Connie to actually see me, I would have been in the Mexican pharmacy buying them on my own."

But I had so much fun with Doctor Connie when she did walk in.

I had recognized her when I opened the door to the examining room and walked out when the waiting was getting to me. And she looked like such a lively beautiful fun woman.

I'm not sure if she recognized me instantly altho when I said "hi!" enthusiastically she said "hi" back in real friendly way and said "I will be with you in a second."

"Good!" I said.

My Higher Self had suggested I bring my books for her in a little bag and give them to her as soon as she walks in.

So as soon as she walked in I took them out of the bag and put them on the table and asked her if she likes to read.

She said yes but usually she is too busy.

So I said "These are books I wrote. They are for you. But this one is the little children's book my dad wrote for me when I was 4 years old."

She got so excited. She said "I have a little daughter."

"Great!" I said.

Then I showed her my little womens lib book and said "this one is a lot of fun."

And she picked up the childrens book and little womens lib book and said "I'll give them to my daughter."

I giggled and said "I don't think you want to give the womens lib book to your 4 year old daughter. You know we did talk about sex in womens liberation, I think your daughter is too young to hear about orgasms."

I was laughing but she actually recoiled in shock. I was surprised that a lady doctor would be so shocked by the word orgasm.

"O no!" she instantly said when I said she is too young to hear about orgasms.

But she was very interested in the little childrens book my dad wrote for me.

Back in New York my friend Irene had done a drawing to go with each of the poems, they are all fairy tales.

Because the liveliest of Irene's drawings is the one for Rumpelstiltskin, I put that one on the cover.

"Is this your dad?" Dr Connie asked.

"No" I said "that is Rumpelstiltskin."

Irene's drawing of Rumpelstiltskin on cover

It's not Dr Connie's fault. I am a writer and publisher. A year after I published my little womens lib book where the women talk about orgasms, I decided to publish the poems my father wrote for me when I was 4 years old.

I am used to going back and forth between Cinderella and orgasms, but for Dr Connie it was too much....

February 28th afternoon

I went to court this morning

Anne shows up at court

The cop had said to me I am giving you two tickets. One for driving in the bike lane and the other for expired license.

And he handed me the paper with the two citations on it

and little booklet with it.

Last week when I was very early after my swim at Y waiting for Jim to get me and it was too cold to wait outside, I sat in the waiting room and got out the citations and the booklet.

The booklet had some of the citations on it. For expired license it said $70 but if you go down and get another license and show that to the judge you don't have to pay it.

And since I had taken the written test the day after the tickets and gotten my new learners permit I saw I wouldn't have to pay that one.

But the other one driving in bike lane, the citation number with it wasn't on the booklet. So I had no idea how much that ticket would be.

At the bottom of the citation it said to go to court on February 28th, and court opens at 8 am and it gave the address.

So yesterday I said to Jim, "Pick me up at 7:30 so I can be there at 8 when it opens.

"I'll probably finish at 10 so you can pick me up then and we can both go swimming."

I woke up at 6 am this morning and even tho I wanted to go back to sleep I realized I have to get ready for court.

Yesterday I had painted my fingernails to look pretty for the judge. And of course all day I kept saying to myself what I will say to the judge.

So I forced myself to get up at 6 am, fed the kitties, put up my coffee, and organized for court.

I had my checkbook and my credit card so I could pay whatever it comes to. Plus I found 2 dollar bills, I put that in my change purse, along with two 20 dollar bills.

I changed my outfit a few times, I wanted to look nice but I didn't want to wear a bra.

And I got out the new pretty heels I had bought at Payless last week.

At 6:30 I called Jim and woke him up. "Can you be here at 7:30?"

"Yes" he said.

I only got to have few sips of my coffee.

I reorganized my pocketbook so I would be sure to have all the paperwork for court. I had one minute before Jim drove into my driveway so I rushed out to paint my toenails.

And I put my swim bag, towel, and bathing suit in truck too for after court.

"When we go to court" I said, "you don't have to come

in with me, I am not afraid to talk to the judge.

"Why don't you go to your club and have wonderful jacuzzi, steam, and sauna and schmooze with your friends.

"Come back for me at 10 o'clock or 10:15, I am sure I will be finished then."

Going in thru the metal detector was so much fun, and I was laughing with the girl security guard in charge.

And she pointed to the courtroom for traffic tickets.

The line was so tiny because I was so early. So I asked the man ahead of me if he could hold my place so I could go to the ladies room.

He said "of course." But just then they opened the door, and he even let me ahead of him. What a gentleman!

The lady said "Go to window 5."

I was so surprised because I expected to walk into a court room.

I couldn't figure it out. Are the judges behind the windows and I tell them the story?

But at Window 5 was a very nice girl. I showed her my citation. She looked them both up on her computer.

She said "You can pay it all now or go to defensive driving school or see a judge."

I said "how much is the driving in bike lane one?"

She looked on her computer and said "199."

Plus I have to see the judge to show him I got my learners permit again and take away that fine.

So I said "I want to see the judge."

So she said "Fill out this paper. And you will get something in the mail in two weeks giving you an appointment to see the judge in a month."

"I didn't know that, no one told me that. I thought I would see the judge today. It is only ten after 8 and my friend won't come to pick me up till 10 o'clock. I don't have cell phone. Where can I call him?"

Her cell phone was right by her on her desk, along with her half eaten bagel. I hoped she would offer to call Jim.

But instead she said "I will show you where the pay phones are, meet me at the end of this."

She was very nice and took me down the hall and pointed out ladies room for me and public phones.

Luckily I saw I had a few quarters in my change purse. I didn't know where to call Jim. On his cell phone or call him at Racquet Club?

I decided to do his cell phone first in case he went home and not to Club.

I put in my quarter but it kept asking for 25 cents.

So I hung up and tried again.

And same thing happened

So I thought I don't know how to operate this public telephone.

I went into an office and told the girl behind the desk the whole story. Her cell phone was sitting right there, I hoped she would offer. When she didn't I said "how do the public phones work?"

She said "I have no idea."

I was standing there totally flummoxed, I did not know what to do.

A cop came in and immediately began chatting with her. He was so enthusiastic to be there and chat with her.

And he was showing her pictures and games on his cell phone.

So I told him my story that I need help with the public telephone.

At some point I must have been near tears from all my frustration and desperation so my voice got louder with emotion.

He immediately ordered me "DON'T YELL AT ME!"

I probably hit bottom then.

I knew he was not going to help me. Instead he jeered at

me when I said "I put in my quarter."

He said "pay phones have not been a quarter for 20 years."

"How much are they now?" I asked

"I don't know" he said, "35 cents."

And then he taunted me. Making fun of my New York City accent. Imitating it.

Then he went back to showing her all the things on his cell phone. He was so happy talking to her.

I saw 3 telephone books on a shelf on the side and hoped I could find the phone number for Racquet Club. I was so glad when I found it. And folded the phone book to that page to take to the public phone.

"Where are you going with that phone book!" he barked at me.

"I am just taking it to public phone. I will bring it back. I am not stealing it."

Everything was crazy at the public phone. It said put in 4 quarters for 4 minutes.

So I put in 4 quarters and dialed Racquet Club. The book must have been out of date. Instead what I got was a recording asking "What is your emergency? Are you dying? Are you having a heart attack?"

I hung up and hoped my money would be returned. It was not.

Then I saw it said 50 cents for local call. I had two quarters left. I called Jim's cell phone.

When it rang 5 times I knew he is not at home but at the Club and since he never picks up his messages I hung up before the recording began "leave a message," hoping my quarters would be returned. They were not.

I brought the phonebook back and the policeman was still showing her everything on his cell phone. Calling out the names of cities, "San Antonio" and "San Diego" etc.

So I decided to go outside and have a cigarette.

I could not find any place to sit down and kept crossing streets. Finally I saw a place with a lot of benches. And went there.

It turned out to be the bus terminal. "Fine" I thought, "I will take the bus home."

It was about twenty to nine now. They had clock showing the time. When a bus pulled up I asked the driver "which is the bus to Swan and 5th?

He said "behind me."

I walked up and down looking at all the buses and the ones pulling in, but none of them were the right bus for me, they were all going someplace else.

When a bus pulled in and opened the door I saw "exact change needed."

I said "how much does it cost?"

He said "1.50."

I said "I have two dollars."

I had checked my change purse. He said "that is fine."

Finally I sat down on a bench, altho it was so cold in the shade. The bench in the sunshine was all filled up.

I saw a teenager with his cell phone. I debated for a while and then summoned up my courage. I had 20 cents left. I said I can give it to him if I can call my friend and say pick me up.

He said "I have no minutes left."

I could tell he thought I was a panhandler and was trying to get rid of me.

But then a nice miracle happened. A girl who was also standing there said she is also waiting for the Number 3 bus. And it is supposed to be arriving now and she doesn't know where it is.

She said "I am just going to take it to the other side of the tunnel. I could walk there but it is so cold in the tunnel."

You have to go thru a tunnel to get into or leave downtown.

She said "The bus is supposed to be here now. And my class is at 9 o'clock."

The clock said 5 to nine.

I said "I sure hope it comes so you are not late for class."

She said "It is OK my boyfriend knows I am late."

She said "That is our bus now but it has to pull around."

She sure knew her way around the buses.

And when it pulled around she got on right away. I said to the driver "I have two singles." And he pointed to the thing to put them both in. And they slid thru nicely.

I was so happy to be on the bus. I forgot I love buses and haven't been on one for almost 20 years. My first year in Tucson I took it twice when Bill did not want to drive me to the mall.

The back of the bus was elevated, you step up two steps. Of course I wanted to sit up high.

So I went to the last seat in last row in back of bus and sat by the window so I could look out.

And after the tunnel at the first stop I looked out the window and there was my friend from the bus terminal.

I knocked on the window with my rings. She looked up

and saw me and waved to me and I waved to her. I couldn't understand what school she went to, I didn't see any school.

But the friendliness made me happy.

I actually was completely happy during my bus ride. It was fun he went so slowly so I could look around. Jim drives so fast and is mainly mad at other drivers who hold him up.

Then I noticed the teenage boy sitting on the side seat. He had his magic markers out and was doing a tattoo on his hand. I found that so interesting to watch.

Then he got out his cell phone and used it as a mirror and combed his long hair and made it into a hair-do he liked. His hair was chin length. He shook it so it fell the way he liked. And studied it in his cell phone mirror.

I watched him for a long time, it was so interesting how he was making himself beautiful. Plus I loved looking out the window too.

Then a beautiful girl got on and that was so exciting. She was blond with glasses but her glasses made her even more beautiful. And I noticed she had black fishnet stockings and boots. She looked so alive. She was a joy to look at.

She had enormous purse. And first she took out the

tablet and did a few things with it. She used it as a mirror too. She pursed her lips and looked at herself.

Then she went into her enormous pocketbook and pulled out a paperback book. It was big, as big as my books. And I was so gratified to see someone still does read books.

Then my Higher Self said "Look away! You can't keep looking at her, it is called staring and it is rude."

So I forced my eyes off her and looked out the window again. I guess it was OK with the teenage boy because he was unaware of me, he was in his own world. He had now taken out two notebooks, but they had writing on cover.

I didn't know what it was about.

So I looked out the window all the way till we reached Columbus Road which is the road before mine, mine is Swan.

At first I couldn't figure out how you let the driver know you want him to stop. I know how you do it in NYC, you just pull the thing. But I didn't see the thing to pull and thought "maybe you press a button" but I didn't see a button.

But then I saw the thing to pull on other side of the bus, so looked up and there was one on my side too. Low down.

So after Columbus I pulled it. But to my surprise he made a stop in between before he got to my street. He thought that was what I wanted.

So I walked up to the front of the bus and said "I'm so sorry. I made a mistake. I'm going to Swan."

There was another bus driver standing next to him schmoozing the whole time.

When I said "I'm going to Swan" he said "are you going to Codac?"

"Why" I said and burst out laughing, "do I look like a mental patient!"

I was laughing at my joke, I found it so funny.

My dog always used to take me to the Codac parking lot. It is near my house. She would go up to everybody and kiss them. Some of the people looked like they had not cracked a smile in 20 years. But they were happy when my dog gave them love. That's how I knew it was some kind of therapy center.

The parking lot is always full so I realize they have to show up once a month to renew their prescription.

Just when I was going to get off the bus a girl in front said to the driver she just wants to get off for a second to throw her tissue out.

"Hand it to me" I said, "I will put it in garbage can for you."

She gave me her tissue and I was still laughing at my joke and happy to do a favor.

So I hopped out in such a good mood and threw the tissue in the garbage can right next to bench at bus stop.

I went home as fast as I could and rushed in the house so I could call Jim before he left to pick me up at court.

I tried his cell phone twice, no answer. But I figured he would realize I was home when my name showed up.

Then I looked up Racquet Club on my computer. I asked the guy at the desk if Jim is there. And the guy said yes.

I said "Tell him Annie is home. Don't go to court. The judge would not see her."

He said he will give Jim the message.

Then I changed into my play clothes so I could rush outside with my comforter and lay in the sunshine.

I also heated up the coffee I never got to drink in the morning.

Jim called. "I'm home" I said. "I took the bus. They wouldn't let me see the judge.

"Come to my house, we will decide about swimming then."

I rushed off the phone because I really wanted to get to that glorious sunshine and lie down and drink my coffee.

I was surprised it took Jim so long to arrive. I thought "well maybe he is doing errands."

But when he did arrive, it turned out he had been at court for a long time looking for me. When I wasn't outside, he had parked, put in his quarter. And went inside. And went upstairs to all the judge's chambers to see if I was there.

And then he got my call on his cellphone.

I felt terrible that I had not been able to reach him in time.

He was sitting in my backyard in the sunshine petting my cat Priscilla who was in ecstasy at all his loving wonderful pets and rubs.

I told him my whole story from beginning to end.

He wasn't interested in my story except for what happened about the appointment with seeing the judge.

All he said when I finished my story was "well at least you got home."

I said "Jim I discovered I love taking the bus. I wished I could take the bus everywhere. So now we know when I have to go to court to see the judge, you can take me there.

But when it is over I can cross the street to the bus terminal and take bus home.

"You don't have to pick me up."

I had gotten out all my magic markers after he called, and decided when he arrives I will have him draw a tattoo on my back.

I have been dying for a tattoo for 20 years. Watching the guy on the bus draw a tattoo on back of his hand with magic markers gave me good idea.

I showed Jim the magic markers and said "Make a flower. It doesn't have to be good because when I get out of the pool it will be gone."

So he drew a flower on my back with my magic markers. He did it in 4 seconds!

I wasn't going to go swimming, I thought I had enough adventures for one day.

When I was lying in the sunshine waiting for Jim to come, my Higher Self said, "You had a great experience." She said, "A great experience means tears and laughter and all new experiences."

I was surprised She called it a great experience because some of it was bad, but I let Her talk me into it.

Jim said he has to go back to his club anyway because he

left his swim bag there. So I said "OK I may as well take my swim."

It was so nice arriving and seeing the familiar and wonderful girls behind the desk, and then going in the pool and wonderful Nancy and sweet lifeguard. And I told them the whole story and showed them my tattoo.

I said "I hope it is a flower but you never know what someone does behind your back," and I burst out laughing.

They said "it is a pretty flower."

I only got to swim a little because I arrived so late and was chatting with Nancy and lifeguard. But the last 5 minutes was great and the hot shower was great.

I said to Nancy "I have to be lickety-split because Jim is coming at noon and after what I put him thru this morning I don't want to make him wait."

And Jim was there when I got out and we had fun in the car.

I told him "I showed everyone your tattoo and they loved it."

And he looked and said, "There is nothing there now. After all my hard work."

I said "Next time draw a scary rattlesnake and we'll take picture of it.

"I'll send the pic to my friends on email, they won't know it is magic markers.

"I will say 'here I am with my new tattoo.'"

He got into it. He said "I'll draw one with fangs and blood dripping from his fangs."

"Fine!" I said, "I will tell my friends the best tattoo artist in Tucson did it."

And he laughed at being called a tattoo artist.

So I guess all's well that ends well.

I sure was happy girl when he dropped me off and headed right back to my sunshine with my ice cold orange soda.

After court I swim with my new tattoo

Glorious Spring

The earth has risen and so has Anne

We drive to Sandra's house

Maybe today was a lucky day because I just found my 3rd email of someone reporting their good news today.

It had such a good effect on me. I get encouraged when I hear good news. My optimism always goes up a notch.

I had a lazy Sunday afternoon. After I got back from swimming I napped in front of TV.

Before swimming I had Jim drive me to the house of a girl who grew up in my housing project in Flushing, Pomonok.

I met her in the Pomonok Group on FaceBook and it turns out she lives in Tucson now. She arrived here 10 years after me.

She had posted to me on FaceBook that she wanted to buy one of my books, so I posted back to her I will bring them to her if she emails me her address.

So I put them all in a shopping bag this morning and

gave Jim her address.

She said she will be doing bird photography this morning so leave them on the bench by her door.

Her address meant nothing to me, nor her directions. I assumed she lived here in town like me.

But Jim recognized the names of the streets where she said "hang a right."

LOL it turned out to be out in the Tucson mountains way west of me. In a fancy new development with a country club.

Jim did not enjoy the long drive, but I thought it was fun being driven somewhere else other than to my Y or to supermarket or pet food or credit union.

It is desert mountains, all cactus. I liked it.

Of course if she does read any of my books she will find out what a nut I am.

In the Pomonok Group we just post about our childhood in Pomonok. The games we all played or our teacher in 6th Grade.

I try to act like a normal Pomonok girl.

But I was not back then. I was not one bit like the other girls in my class, all from Pomonok.

LOL and I am far weirder now than I ever was then.

And I have the impression that Sandra is not one bit weird.

Well we will see. At least now she knows I am a writer and hopefully she believes all writers are weird. And I will get a pass on that basis.

A very bad cat came in from the alley yesterday to eat my cats' food.

It wasn't Muggles. It was *The Son of Muggles*.

As he was leaving the house he spotted Priscilla and chased her all the way up to the top of the tree in front of my window.

He is not welcome to come back!

She slept with me all night in my back bedroom because of the bad experience she had that evening.

Some of those alley cats are bullies!!

The one who comes every day for breakfast lunch and supper behaves like a gentleman.

I wish you all a lovely evening and sweet dreams.

Love Annie

Post script, the next day Sandra invites me to lunch

The next day I got an email from Sandra offering to take me to lunch. I assumed it was because she started to read one of my books and decided she liked me.

But maybe when someone gives you a whole shopping bag of their books as a gift, a person thinks they have to give you a gift in return. Offering to take me to lunch was Sandra's gift in return.

I didn't expect a gift in return. I am always thrilled when anyone wants to read any of my books. Even if they don't like them, I hope they pass them on to someone else. I just want my books to be read..

I was trepidatious about our lunch date. I knew she was expecting a regular Pomonok girl like herself, and if there is anything I am not, it is a regular Pomonok girl.

I postponed our lunch until my court thing-y was all over. But finally in late Spring the day for our lunch arrived.

We arranged she would pick me up after my morning swim at the Y and drive us to Village Inn a mile away.

I remember being nervous during my swim. I said to Emily the girl lifeguard, "I never met her but she grew up around the corner from me."

Emily said "I think it will be nice for you Anne, you will be seeing someone from home."

"That's true" I said. "I barely have any family, it will be nice to see someone from home."

Lunch with Sandra

Anne is trepidatious, but hopes for the best

Lunch with Sandra Weiser began off worse than I ever could have imagined. The first thing she said to me when we were first seated at Village Inn was "You dress weird. You talk weird. You act weird. You are totally weird!

"Does your family talk to you?"

"My brother and my cousins never call."

"I can see why!" she said.

I realized she had steered me away from the nice booth by the window, to the small table in dark corner away from everyone, so my weirdness would not bother our fellow luncheon ladies.

I had forgotten about being weird because Bill and I had lived in the East Village of lower Manhattan which is a neighborhood of misfits. It had been the hippy neighborhood in the '60s and I moved there then and never left.

It wasn't only hippies and misfits it was also the immigrants who never bettered themselves.

LOL what we all had in common was no image to uphold and no success.

We were the ones our parents cried about when their friends asked "how is Annie doing?"

As my friend Ellen Goldfarb said — She lived around the corner from me in the East Village. Her mother still lived in the Bronx where Ellen grew up.

Ellen told me, "My mother called. She said yesterday I saw Mrs. Katz outside the supermarket and she asked me about you and I had to run away with my shopping cart."

I loved my neighborhood, we were all so nice to each other and tried to help each other. And it was so relaxing to live there.

I did wonder what it would be like for me when I moved to Tucson. Would it be like living in Flushing all over again. And I would have to go back to trying to fit in.

I don't know what other places are like, I have only lived in NYC and Tucson, but Tucson is all love and nothing but love. I am completely happy here.

I wondered how I was going to make it thru lunch when Sandra started off with how weird I am. And had apoplexy in the car about me not wearing a bra when she had met me at the Y and driven us over for lunch at Village Inn.

But the tide turned when she told me how last year her husband had a heart attack on his country club golf course and by a great miracle, a doctor who never golfs on Fridays had been golfing that Friday and was right there and saved her husband.

It was such trauma for her that now she is scared to death everytime her husband goes in for routine test for anything.

She said "Tomorrow he goes in for his test for" (I forget what now) and to my surprise she started to cry. "I am so scared.

"If anything happens to him I don't know what I will

do."

I understand loving your husband with all your heart, and Sandra has been with him since they were childhood sweethearts.

Sandra had had a terrible frown on her face from instant she saw me standing outside the Y. She thought I was total kook and was probably wondering how she would get thru this lunch.

I saw that frown and thought "this is not going to be easy."

However that frown face dissolved into tears about her husband's test the next day. That was it. I loved Sandra with all my heart.

I took her hand and held it and let my Higher Self speak words of love and comfort thru me to her. I told Sandra "This is my Higher Self speaking to you, not me."

And Sandra let me do it. And my Higher Self promised her that Marty was fine and would always be fine and she has nothing to worry about at all. And poured all Her love into Sandra.

And of course that changed everything. We both melted towards the other.

And after lunch Sandra took her fancy expensive camera

that she uses when she goes bird watching with her husband, and took photos of Bill's art all over my walls so I could send them to Bill's sister, and took the photo of Irene's painting which is up on my wall too.

I was able to send that to the girls in my womens lib group who all know Irene and also to Irene's big brother when I got on email with him recently.

And Sandra was sweet enuf to send me a thank you email when she got back the doctor's report of the test that Marty is fine.

"He is fine just as you promised Anne," she said.

I don't think Sandra and I will ever try to have lunch together again, it was too big a stretch for both of us.

But I think each of us knows we have a friend in our corner with each other. I would do anything for Sandra and she would do anything for me.

Sunday March 24

Wonderful driving lesson this morning...

I love the animals in the countryside

I had divine driving lesson this morning. Jim took me to the country. It was fun driving fast on the empty deserted road after 2 weeks of creeping along my own neighborhood for half hour before swimming.

It felt like actually driving moving along so fast. But the 2 weeks of slow neighborhood driving did pay off. I was relaxed and confident behind the wheel. And that was great for me.

LOL my life is all extremes these days. Either 10 miles an hour in my own neighborhood, or speeding along on the deserted empty country road.

I was happy to be doing it and it made Jim happy too. He liked it that I was finally going fast.

I drove to the end of Swan Road, did 3 tushy turns to practice for the road test, and Jim was thrilled when I actually took my hands off the wheel during the last one.

It is so much fun for me when he has confidence in me as a driver. LOL it happens so rarely. Maybe never.

On the way back up Swan Road, again I was going at a very fast clip, when suddenly I saw a bull lying down by the side of the road. Or maybe he was standing there.

"I am driving off the road so I can watch" I said to Jim.

"O no we will get gored!" he said.

I didn't appreciate it that he frightened me because for me it was love at first sight. But the result is I did pull up a little away from the bulls instead of right by them.

Because it turned out there were 7 of them lying down

on the other side of the road. And my heart just went wild with joy.

It is the most beautiful sight I ever saw in my life. I have no idea why and there simply is no explanation. Why 7 bulls lying down all beside each other should have been such total and complete and passionate beauty for me.

The love which rose in me was just tremendous. I couldn't stop drinking in the sight.

I had to crane my neck the whole time to look thru that small area where the back windows in the truck open up and I kept looking and looking.

I just kept drinking in the sight. I couldn't get enuf of it. Finally I said to Jim "it's better than sex."

I meant it. It was surfeit of bliss.

I couldn't believe that I was this fortunate to have this divine experience.

After that I drove to the traffic light. And drove to the next light. We switched seats so Jim could drive us back to town

"Stop at Nico's so I can get a fish taco" I said.

"Are you going swimming?" he asked

"Might as well" I said

But after we got close to my house I changed my mind.

My outing had been so satisfying. It was beautiful day to boot. I had my fish taco on the dashboard, I was hungry.

I said "I think I'll just go home, have my taco, my soda, and my cigs in my back yard. You're free all day to do exactly what you want."

And I did have my taco, soda, and cigs in my backyard. It was only noon, and for the rest of the day I didn't know what to do with myself.

I was like a jitterbug. Lounging on comforter in backyard didn't work. Watching TV did not work. Coming in here to my computer did not work.

Nothing held my interest.

And my thoughts were the worst jitterbug of all. They just jumped around. LOL in some meaningless jitterbug dance.

I guess the nice thing about my driving lesson, not up there with seeing the bulls of course, which was a divine experience for me, was how well Jim and I got along.

We don't always get along, sometimes we bug each other and get on each other's nerves.

In fact yesterday was one of those days.

But this morning maybe for the first time ever we were on the same page. Everything we said pleased the other.

We couldn't agree more.

We got along splendidly.

And who knows maybe this was the source of the great happiness for both of us all thru the driving lesson from beginning to end.

From instant he picked me up till he dropped me off, the getting along had been smooth as silk. And we had never had that before.

We were both in an up mood and pleased with each other.

Maybe Jim was pleased with life. Everything he told me he was glad about.

And of course I was so glad he was glad. It made me glad.

Ordinarily communication between us is simply nil. We live in 2 different worlds. And they are too opposite to ever mesh. We solve it by tuning each other out constantly.

Whatever I say he tunes me out. Whatever he says I tune him out.

LOL if neither of us is quick enuf on the draw to tune each other out before we heard what the other person says, we go into irritation mode.

It's amazing this beautiful friendship between us exists.

Maybe because we each help the other out so much and both know we have each others best interests at heart. It provides the springs for our friendship.

We muddle thru without too many jostles and bumps.

We do get along.

It's rare that we don't.

But today was the icing on the cake. It was not just getting along, it was pure joy in each others company.

It may be as rare as seeing 7 bulls all lying together by the side of road and drinking in all that beauty, but who cares.

They were both a great gift and made for a spectacular morning.

Email March 26th

Jim throws his wallet in garbage can

I was late for swimming and had such short time because Jim spent 3 hours looking for the car keys.

I had tried to tell him we are in a higher Dimension now and the mind won't work the same on automatic pilot the way it used to.

You have to pay attention when you do things. LOL because when you're not paying attention the mind doesn't carry it out on its own.

In this case he stopped to pick up his mail when he drove into his driveway, put the keys down on hood of car, and stood there reading his mail.

So tearing up his house for 3 hours and looking in every drawer in the house did not make the keys show up.

Last week he spent 7 hours looking for his wallet. He was just about to call and cancel his credit cards when he discovered it in the garbage.

And it happened again the next day!

And few days after that with his cell phone!

He has spent a lot of time looking for misplaced items and upsetting himself very much.

But of course he tunes me out when I say about the new Dimension.

He thinks I am crackpot.

I notice I have to remind myself about everything. For instance if I am watching tv in back bedroom and realize I did not bring in my cordless phone with me.

Not that anyone ever calls me, but the last thing I want to do is race thru the house to answer the phone.

As I walk thru the kitchen I decide to fix myself an ice cold soda to take back to tv with me. But if I do not actually remind myself that what I came in for was my phone, I would return without it.

I have to remind myself about everything like that now.

I actually have to pay attention to all the things I always did automatically before.

Maybe in this new Dimension we have to be more attentive or we will throw our wallet in the garbage :)

Love Annie

April 2

(from Ruthie who now lives in Hawaii)

From: Ruthie
To: Anne, Pat, Peggy, Jean, Heather, Jo, Casey
Subject: Anne's altered state..

oh dear oh dear-

i quite understand those ups downs all arounds

would make one dizzy me thinks

all going so fast don't know if i can stay on the boat-

not exactly smooth sailing.

when the waves get real choppy..

we're all having headaches and exhaustion here-

we think it's the VOG

(sulfur coming over from the big island volcano going

off)

and then suddenly a lovely day

need the sailors stomach

I love this email from Ruthie.

Because that is what today was *and then suddenly a lovely day.*

The beauty of the day was so lovely.

The water in the pool was so lovely.

The friendly conversation going on in the pool was so lovely.

I looked up at the blue sky and thought *"Today is a day made for happiness."*

We were all so happy at the pool today

April 3rd

My strange birthday

Something weird is going on. I don't know what it is because it is not something which has happened before.

First of all I slept too much last night. Who falls asleep at 8 pm and sleeps all the way to morning!

Usually when I've had a long nap in the afternoon if I fall asleep at 8 pm, I am up for few hours in middle of the night.

The other thing is my dreams were different. I don't remember how or why. They just were. I only remember one of them now. I was driving a car, it was an automatic.

I had never driven an automatic before. My truck is the clutch. It all seemed so easy, I didn't have to do any work.

It seemed to drive itself. And it went fast too.

The other odd thing is I seem to have twisted my foot while I slept. Who twists their foot while they sleep! But this morning I am hobbling.

Yesterday was such a gloriously happy day, the last thing I expected was to wake up this morning and wonder how am I going to get around if I can only hobble.

I was so dismayed.

To lift my spirits I thought "tomorrow is my birthday why don't I see if Baik Baik (my favorite designer) has pretty new skirts for spring."

So I went back into the house (I had been lying in sunshine in backyard) and looked on her website.

There were three I liked of her new spring skirts, and one on sale from last year.

I knew no one would be in the office in Honolulu so I left the message on the machine.

"It's my birthday" I said. "For my birthday present to myself I want to buy your pretty new skirts. Can you call me back when it is convenient for you. Love Annie in Tucson."

When I got off the phone I was thrilled. I knew it came to $300 altogether but I decided to throw money to the wind. Never in my whole life did I throw money to the wind. Never in my whole life did I expect to.

But I thought, It is an emergency. I didn't want to be so unhappy on my birthday. I wanted to be lifted up, and buying myself the pretty new skirts did even more than that.

It reversed the funk I was falling into and made life wonderful. I was getting such fabulous birthday presents.

And I hobbled back to my comforter on the ground in the sunshine. And thought "what a strange morning, maybe it means something wonderful is coming into my life."

A brand new optimism opened up before me.

Post script

I completely forgot that I thought my life was going to change for the better because for the rest of that day and the next two days it changed so much for the worse!

Whatever booboo started up in my foot while I slept increased so much that by the evening I couldn't walk on it.

I spent the afternoon and evening back in the tool room again while the cooler technician set up my coolers for the summer.

He was an angel to me.

Both he and his boss when his boss came over to help him were angels.

I tried to get up when his boss came over but nearly fell over.

By 9 pm the discomfort had been so relentless for two hours, I called up Jim. "My ibuprofen is in my back bedroom but I can't walk there to get it. Will you come over to bring it to me?"

Jim was already in bed. "Let me get dressed I'll be right over."

He brought me my ibuprofen and an iced cold 7 Up from the frig.

And petted and loved Priscilla who was lying on the dresser next to me.

Jim saved me. It wasn't only the ibuprofen and soda. He broke the spell of the worry that I had fallen into. The discomfort itself was barely noticeable, it just worried me so much that I could not walk.

I had to break out of that gloom. And Jim's arrival and help did all that for me.

From the moment he walked in the door I switched gears and relaxed. And when he left I thought "well maybe it will all be OK."

April 6th early morning

My Higher Self Interprets my Dream

Susan is my friend in New York City

Before I woke up this morning I had long dream about Susan Doretsky who was my best friend before I left NYC. In the dream I was back in her apt. in NYC. She was talking on the telephone. I don't know if she was aware I was there.

She was having a long conversation with what appeared like very close friend who shared her life with her. In my dream Susan did all the talking.

Since in real life she won't return my phone calls and is not on email. So in the dream at first I was miffed that she won't talk to me on the phone.

I thought "Aha she tells me she doesn't like to talk on the telephone. But now I see with my own eyes she does like long conversation on the phone. So it is just me that she doesn't want to hang out with on the phone."

But then I realized "So what if she doesn't want to talk to me on the phone, I am hearing everything she wants to say anyway. I get to hear it all because I am here listening. So it is just as well. I am getting the long phone call this way."

And I did find every bit of her phone call interesting. Not because of anything particular she said, I just wanted to hear her express herself.

Maybe I was staying over at her house. I know when it was time for me to leave I looked all over for my pink swim bag.

Susan didn't seem to be aware that I was there. I hadn't wanted to make my presence known.

I was in another room listening to her phone call.

But I had to interact with her when I couldn't find my swim bag. I had to show myself. I tried to describe it to her. "It is pink with a pink ballerina on it."

We both looked all over but it was nowhere to be found. "OK" I thought, "I will go back without it, but too bad I like that swim bag. I used it. What will I use now to put my wet bathing suit in after my shower."

But then to my surprise it showed up in her car as I was leaving. I was so surprised because I didn't think I had taken it to the car. I didn't think she had a car.

But I was glad to see it and take it back. I was glad to have found it.

The reason I came out of my hiding place and into view is I wanted to say to her, "Now that we are both so slender now"— (she had been fat when I last saw her in NYC before I moved to Tucson and I had gotten fat in Tucson. But I looked at her now, she might even be slenderer than me and I have gotten slender myself)— I said "We can trade clothes. You give me what you no longer want to wear and I will give you my clothes. It will be fun for both of us."

Interpretation of dream by my Higher Self

I take down Her words as she says them to me

This is actually an important dream Anne had.

Altho she forgot to put in the last part. In her dream at the very end Susan was concerned if she ran out of money where would she live.

Susan's friend said "you can live with me."

And Anne said "I have a big house now with a lot of rooms. And I am used to living with someone.

"When I lived in it with Bill it wouldn't have worked if you lived with us too. But now you are more than welcome to come live in it with me whenever you want.

"Altho if you want your own place, I have a huge backyard if you are willing to live in a trailer.

"A trailer would be the same size as your little apartment now.

"We could put your trailer in a beautiful spot way in the back of my backyard and you could have your own home there."

In fact that is the real reason Anne came out of hiding and made her appearance known to Susan. She wanted to offer Susan her home if for some reason Susan did not have her home in NYC.

Since Anne read in her *Letter From God* yesterday that everyone you meet or encounter in the world is really yourself and how you get to know yourself, then obviously Susan is Anne.

She is seeing herself projected outwards.

Susan is the emblem of Anne's New York self. Susan is the quintessential New Yorker. She is gregarious. She is talkative. She is communicative. She has close friends. They talk about their lives together. They share everything. They like expressing themselves.

Anne sees that Susan has a nice bag but she wants her own pink ballerina bag back. She loves the pink ballerina bag and uses it all the time. It is also practical.

At first when Anne can't find it anywhere she thinks she lost it and will have to do without it but then by miracle it shows up in Susan's car.

This is quite a stretch since she has never been in Susan's car plus in real life Susan does not even have a car.

So it counts as a miracle. Something precious and loved; something wonderful and beautiful and pink. With a ballerina on it, is found. What was lost is found.

The beautiful ballerina sailing thru the air with her legs outstretched.

The important thing of course is Anne's generosity to Susan. Her offer of gifts. "We are the same size now, I can give you my clothes. Even if you lose your home you can have a home with me. Either share my house or I can make you a home of your own in my beautiful backyard in the midst of beautiful nature."

With trees and the bird song.

And peace and quiet.

My darling Anne I know this has been a very rough week for you. Easter Sunday which always was your favorite holiday, instead of it being a day in paradise, was a total bitch for you. And the next day was tough too.

Then you had your happy day in beautiful paradise.

And then 3 days which were so tough they bordered on misery. And those 3 days were the days of your birthday. The day before your birthday, the day of your birthday, the day after your birthday.

So the idea of Happy Easter and Happy Birthday got

ruined for you. No longer will you look forward to either one.

Now you see both of them like Christmas, a day you just hope to get thru painlessly and will be so glad when it is finally over and so relieved it only arrives once a year.

LOL holidays are ruined for you.

But my darling try to see that all your love devotion appreciation and generosity and consideration of Susan actually means a new relationship with yourself.

Honeybunch this is really what has been going on since 2013 arrived and all the misery it brought you. It is how the renovation of your relationship with yourself has been taking place.

All those days in bed too uncomfortable to do anything. And a mind as gray as the gray sky when beautiful sparkling Tucson turns gray.

The reason a gray sky in Tucson is much grayer than anywhere else is because that dense gray cloud cover blocks out a sun that is brighter than anywhere else.

The change in illumination is so much greater. It is such dramatic change. The contrast is so great. That is why it seems so dark to you and why you long so much to have your bright light back.

The bright light is your happiness. You are now used to swimming in and walking in happiness.

But even you must realize that your beautiful desert would dry up while waiting for the summer monsoon to bring it its water, its life. There have to be some cool moist days, which is what the cloud cover brings.

And for you all these days of cloud covered mind, and the discomfort which gets you off your feet and under the covers all day, is when your soul searching takes place.

And how can a complete renovation of your relationship with yourself happen, without all this time of you under the covers so your soul can do all this work it must do. It has big job to do. And it is doing it. And be very thankful for it.

It is great gift your soul is doing for you.

Which it tried to show you in your dream. It offered you pretty clothes to wear. A beautiful home to live in. And a wonderful friend who you love and adore.

So let's just be patient and easy going. To the best of your ability. Whatever time your soul needs, let it take its time. However it wants to accomplish it, let it do it her way.

Honey we are talking about your soul, and this is the time of and for your soul. It is her day.

Just know every instant no matter how much day after day follows which is not to your liking, that the greatest gift in the world is now taking place for you now.

If you can't be grateful (which is too much to ask, who can be grateful for day upon day of lousy days!)

But you can see it in truth. And know that something amazing and wonderful is taking place and a great gift is being given you. And you will reap all the happiness from it.

God bless you my sweet darling and God bless everyone you know and encounter and the whole world too.

I love you.

Your Higher Self.

April 21

Buying pot then and now...

Well the big adventure in my life is that yesterday afternoon, to my big surprise, Jan's husband called me to ask for a favor.

Jan is my dearest friend from NYC. She and her husband Harry moved to Tucson the same summer Ruthie moved to Ocean Beach CA.

The desert did not take for Jan and Harry. They had been living in the woods in NY State when they moved to Tucson. And as soon as they sell their house here they will move back to the woods.

But people stopped buying houses at exactly the same time they finally completed the year's labor of getting their house ready for the market. Jan's husband did so much work.

They finally had to take it off the market after several years of it not selling and always lowering the price. But their dream hasn't changed. They still want to get back to the woods.

I rarely see them, but I used to talk to Jan on the telephone once a month.

Because she is New Age like me, we could talk about everything from a New Age point of view, which I totally appreciate as I do not have that with anyone else.

But the last few months brought such unexpected difficulties into their life I haven't heard from her at all.

Which is why I was surprised when her husband called me yesterday afternoon to ask for a favor. To lift their spirits, he wanted to know if my cousin Gloria could buy them a little pot. I was a pot smoker all thru my twenties, but I have not bought any pot since then.

And I only listen with half an ear when Gloria tells me about buying a little pot for herself, she buys such a tiny quantity. I knew last month Chico, the guy who sells it to her, said he doesn't have any now.

And reaching Chico is always a problem. Either Chico doesn't bother calling back or his cell phone is broken.

And when she does reach Chico, and Chico says "I'll call

you back tomorrow and let you know when I get some in." Tomorrow has a different meaning to Chico than to the rest of us. It seems to mean "some day," "eventually."

I did instantly call Gloria to ask her to do the favor. She said she will do it.

"How much is it?" I asked.

"30" Gloria said.

The last time I bought pot which was in 1970 it was $30 for an ounce, so I thought "Wow the price has not gone up." But it turns out that is the price of a quarter of an ounce which is what Gloria buys.

Gloria called me back and said she left the message with Chico. "It's not a matter of *if* I will be able to get the pot for your friends but *when*. You have to be patient."

So I called Harry back and told him that. He is very grateful and very appreciative to Gloria. I suggested he give Gloria 10 dollars for gas since it is such a long drive out there and back. And Harry said not only 10 for gas but he wants to give Gloria another ten for doing him such a wonderful favor.

LOL I can't believe I'm the middle man in a pot deal. Altho it is such a small deal. $30 for a quarter of an ounce.

But when Chico will call Gloria back is anyone's guess.

And then when Chico will actually have some pot to sell is anyone's guess.

I haven't been back in this world of scoring some pot for such a long time, it does seem like a big adventure to me.

Altho back in the Sixties when my boyfriend Alan was buying some pot for us, we went to Ralph's apartment on East 7th Street (in the East Village of Manhattan).

Ralph was a college student at NYU. He kept the plastic baggies of ounce of pot under the floor board in the living room of the teeny tenement apartment.

He would pry up the floor board and take out a lid and Alan would give him the 20 or 25 dollars it was back then. Actually I think it was $15.

There were always a lot of people hanging out in Ralph's apt. We were all college students.

And after Alan bought the pot he would roll a joint and pass it around, and we all sat there stoned listening to the Beatles and the Rolling Stones and Ravi Shankur.

This was 1966.

I guess the way of doing business has changed now. I would offer to go with Gloria when she drives to Chico's to pick up the pot, but the last thing I want to do is sit around Chico's apartment get stoned and listen to music for 3 hours. With everyone else who is there.

But maybe that is not how business is done anymore. It's been a few years since 1966 and we were all young college students.

And Chico does not sound one bit like a college student. His wife is in jail and he has 4 dobermans.

And with Ralph I don't remember Alan calling him. We would just drop over.

Ralph would pry up the floor board, there was a little cavity underneath. Pull out a lid in a plastic baggie, hand it to Alan. Alan would hand him the $15 and we all sat around stoned and listened to the music on the record player for the rest of the afternoon.

Since me and all my friends went to City College which was free and Ralph was going to NYU which was private and cost money. He probably came from a rich family in California who let him go to New York for college.

Rent on those tiny tenement apartments back then was only $50/month. And no one had a car.

Giggle giggle other than paying his tuition, his parents didn't have to pay a penny for their son in college in NYC since Ralph was working his way thru school.

April 26th

Don't forget your pants!

It is a beautiful morning after the full moon last night. The wind blew all day yesterday so the world outside my window this morning is fresh and new and sparkling. It's like waking up in paradise.

A first morning in paradise. The birds are all out. Big pigeons walking across my yard, pecking at the ground as they walk.

The sky is one of the loveliest of blues. Flawless with a wisp of a cloud. The color of a blue diamond, a pure blue with hint of navy in it, but totally lit up the way a diamond would be. Dripping with freshness and newness. Almost alive in its beauty.

And the tree in front of my window, the sun to the east is shining right into it, so it is bathed in that golden light.

The leaves are lit up and turn a translucent green.

The rest of the yard is in such cool colors. A cool blue sky, a cool darkish green. Only the tree right in front of my window is lit up in golden light.

And the small tree behind it too. Both desert trees. Desert trees do not have tall tree trunks. Just a few feet off the ground are all their branches with green leaves.

Their leaves are not thick and glossy, the size of a hand, like northern trees. They are like teeny green feathers.

The leaves are all shaped exactly like teeny green feathers. So naturally there are gazillion of them. There is no such thing as density.

I can look at the tree out my window filled with its tiny green feather leaves and see right thru it to all the trees behind it and the blue sky thru it too. Nothing blocks your view. I can see right thru it to the mountains to the north.

My neighbor Frank painted my computer room last week and did a spectacular job. The walls had turned so yellowed. It had not been painted since Bill and I moved into the house 21 years ago.

It is a total transformation. Frank painted it 2 coats of the whitest white. So the whole room is far brighter than it ever was.

He is such a peach he even picked up my clothes and papers from all over the floor, and stored them neatly in boxes and then washed the floor.

So the room seems twice as big and 1000 times brighter. And he put Bill's paintings all over the walls. He turned it into a room of beauty.

It is a miracle of joy for me to have a beautiful new computer room now. After all when I am not lounging on my bed watching tv, it is where I spend all my time.

And he washed the windows for me too so the light pours in. And the view out all my windows is now crystal clear.

It is just as clear thru the glass now as thru the open window itself. WOW! It has doubled all my views. I love it.

He made it into a pretty room when it had been an eyesore before. It is a gift, a very nice gift, Frank gave me. To give me this pretty computer room.

I feel like Heaven is smiling on me. This most beautiful day of all days, Anne is in her new pretty computer room too.

A gift from Heaven and from my neighbor Frank. And a gift from Bill too, since it was what he wanted to do for me. But he went to Heaven so I used his bank account to pay

Frank to do it.

A gift from Heaven and from my wonderful husband and my wonderful neighbor Frank.

When a girl's husband goes to Heaven and he no longer has to take care of her and do everything for her, Heaven steps in. Heaven takes care of her and arranges for everything to be done for her. She is just as well taken care of as when she had her wonderful husband sharing her home with her.

All the movies and tv shows show the girl distraught when her husband goes to Heaven. But that has not been my experience. Distraughtness never entered the picture for me at all.

The first year was a glorious adventure. Suddenly I had a totally brand new life. Nothing was the same as it had been before. Everything was new. New and different.

And now that my second year has been under way for a month, it seems to me the life of a new bachelorette is having fun all the time. All I do is have fun.

It really is a win win situation.

There is nothing as wonderful as being a wife.

And nothing is as fun as having fun all the time.

Luckily we don't get to choose. Life chooses for us.

My love for my husband hasn't changed, it goes right on increasing and growing the way it always did. I live inside my love for him just as a fish lives inside the ocean. It is the environment I swim in.

That hasn't changed, how can that possibly change. That is what marriage or having a mate is. Your love for them is your whole life, and even tho it is infinite it always increases.

What has changed is how I spend my days. Instead of driving to the swim pool every day with Bill, I go with Jim. And the conversation in the car is different because Jim is just a friend.

Altho just a friend doesn't describe it at all because friendship turns out to be far more interesting and multi faceted than the word implies.

It is a relationship too, but not one bit like husband wife. Giggle giggle maybe it is like two peers.

Marriage is like as if you hold out your hands with fingers apart and then bring both hands together. So each finger on one hand fits into the spaces between the fingers on the other hand. A meshing and a joining. It turns it into a hand clasp.

Both hands are joined together.

Friendship isn't one bit like that. You really have to remember being a child, before you were a teenager and interested in boys.

When your cousin Richie exactly your age was your best friend and you played together all day long during the summers up in the Adirondacks where both your families spent their summer vacation.

It's as if that relationship is re-created with me and Jim. All we do is play together, all we do is have fun together. And we are two equals. Being a wife is accommodating your husband, which is a joy to do because it is how you express your love.

But being a friend is the full expression of your being, which is so much fun, because it is so much fun to be so free.

That is why it harkens back to childhood, the total freedom you give yourself. Your expression is one of freedom. Where with your husband your expression is one of love.

With Jim the relationship is so out in the open and up front, like children playing with each other. It's like I never noticed the warm affection underneath I had for my best friend Jane while I was a child.

I didn't notice it till I was writing about her several years ago. And that was all I noticed. It wasn't obscured by all the games and fun and play. All I saw was warm affection. The intimacy and affection.

It is a bit like that with Jim. We are close, we care about each other, we want the other to be happy. We are both sensitive kind souls. In a way maybe we have turned into each others family.

But what goes on when we are together is all play. And we both love it. It's one game after another. The way two year olds play with each other. Two year olds are too young for real games, so they turn life into a game. One spontaneous game after another.

And that's exactly what Jim and I do when we are both in an up mood.

All that goes on is games. The games wouldn't mean anything to anyone else, they got invented as we went along.

An example would be *Don't forget your pants*. One time Jim was an hour late picking me up at the Y. When he arrived he said it was because when he was getting dressed at Racquet Club to pick me up he couldn't find his pants with wallet and car keys in it anywhere.

I guessed another guy had mistakenly thought it was his pants, shoved it into his locker and locked the locker. Anyway that is what it turned out to be after Jim looking high and low for an hour.

When he arrived to pick me up he said "I'm so late because I lost my pants."

So naturally the next morning when he dropped me off at my pool I called out "Don't lose your pants!"

Which has now turned into "Don't forget your pants today."

We have so many games going on now based on all our experiences that if someone were to get in the car with us they would not understand one word we were talking about.

We play *Officer Jeffries*. Officer Jeffries is the girl cop who gave me 2 tickets and was so mean to me back in February.

Officer Jeffries has many variations to it.

It began off when I said to Jim "She has a glock. You have a glock. She will show you her glock. You will show her your glock. And then you will have hot sex together all night."

The next thing I knew Jim was calling her "my bride."

"I hate your bride" I said to him yesterday in the car.

And I don't remember what I said or did last week when Jim said "you're causing me to get a divorce."

Maybe I said "I am going to tell the judge all the mean things Officer Jeffries did to me."

Altho my favorite Officer Jeffries game is each time he drives into the bike lane (that is what I got the ticket for) I turn around and call out the window "Officer Jeffries where are you! He just drove into the bike lane! Give him a ticket for $270."

When I tease him too much he says "I'm not the one with comprehension problems."

I forget all about that, that Officer Jeffries said to me two times "Do you have comprehension problems?"

I forget it but Jim remembers it.

"I hate your bride," I say when he throws that in my face.

May 2ⁿᵈ

I Go Before the Judge

Back in court for another go at it

It was odd interesting intense crazy and something I don't want to do again.

I didn't spend the week before rehearsing what I was

going to say to the judge because I had already done that back in February when the date on the summons said show up in court on February 28th.

I thought I was going to go before the judge then. And for weeks before, I went thru scenarios in my mind of what I would say to the judge.

But when I showed up at traffic court at 8 am the clerk said "Do you want to pay your fines now, go to traffic school or have a hearing?"

I said "I want a hearing."

So she said "Go home and you will get in the mail the date set for your hearing. It will arrive within 2 weeks."

And sure enough 2 weeks later the letter arrived in the mail saying my hearing was set for April 30th at 2:30 pm.

Since it was almost 2 months away I put it out of my mind. Memorized the date, April 30th, and tacked it up on my bulletin board.

I didn't bring it back into my mind till April was well advanced. The week before I looked on my calendar and saw that it was a Tuesday.

And that morning when Jim was driving me to the pool I said "A week from today is my day in court. It's in the afternoon so we can swim in the morning and you can take me to court in the afternoon."

And from that moment on I was aware of going to court the following week.

But I didn't go back to rehearsing what I was going to say. Instead I just thought about logistics.

I thought Jim doesn't have to sit with me all thru it, he can go swim at his club and pick me up when it's over. I just have to bring quarters for the public telephone and tell him to pick up his messages in case he is swimming when his phone rings.

When the weekend before it arrived, I did start to go to it in my mind, and start saying in my mind what I will say to the judge.

But I really didn't want to do that again. So instead I connected to Judge John in my mind, let him love me. And he said I don't have to do that, he will tell me what to say at the time.

So every time my mind went back to it, I nipped it in the bud, and switched over to just letting him love me.

And the evening before my Higher Self said to me, "Anne the outcome doesn't matter. Whether you have to pay the fine or not doesn't matter. It is a great opportunity for you to go there and send love to everyone. You can bless the court by sending love to everyone. That is all you have to do and that is all that matters."

So that relaxed me. After all sending love in my mind is my favorite thing to do anyway, and easy as pie, and I was relieved to find out the outcome didn't matter at all.

Officer Jeffries who had given me all that trouble, had a partner, a man who looked about 10 years older than her and a lot more experienced.

He had been the one who handed me the two tickets. The first one because my learners permit had expired, "This is for driving without a license," he said.

And the second for driving in the bike lane.

And with it a tiny printed up pamphlet which explained about the tickets.

Which Jim immediately began to study.

He said "I can't find driving in bike lane on here, you have to look it up on your computer.

"But for expired license, they take the fine away if you show the judge you have a new license."

So the next morning he took me down to DMV so I could take my written test again and get a new learners permit.

I hadn't expected I would have to take that test again,

Jim kept insisting "they will just extend it for you."

But he was wrong, I did have to take it again.

So on the spot I took it again.

I was allowed 6 wrong answers, but I got 7 wrong answers so I flunked.

Jim got a new copy of the drivers manual for me and as soon as I got home I read it from beginning to end.

The next morning we went back and I took it again. It was totally suspenseful for me. After 6 wrong answers I knew I couldn't get another one.

But instead of praying I got it right, I just prayed that I wouldn't cry if I got it wrong. "Big deal!" I said to myself, "all it would mean is I have to come back tomorrow and take it again."

Of course I really didn't want to, but neither was I going to ruin my happiness over it.

But by a miracle and all my guesses I did pass. I was elated and Jim took me swimming.

I had my new learners permit and could show it to the judge so that ticket would be taken away.

A week or 2 later when it was so cold and dreary being in the swim pool and Jim wasn't coming for another 1/2 hour I sat in the waiting room of the Y going thru my purse.

This is before I went to court the first time.

I found my two tickets at the bottom of my purse and the little pamphlet with them the man officer had given me. And looked up both my violations in the pamphlet.

For driving without a license it said $70. But if you show the judge you have a valid license the judge will take away your fine.

I could not find driving in the bike lane on it.

Jim told me to look it up on the computer because he hadn't found it there either. But I couldn't find it on the computer either.

When I went to court the first time, the clerk said do I want to pay the tickets, go to traffic school or have a hearing.

"How much are both tickets together?" I asked. I thought if driving without a license is only $70 probably driving in the bike lane will be $35.

But she said "both come to $340."

So I said "I want a hearing."

I did the arithmetic after I left her and realized they were going to charge me $270 for the bike lane.

I wanted to show her my new learners permit, but she

said "show it to the judge."

My Afternoon in Court

Jim dropped me off in front of the court house a little before 1:30 and my Higher Self said "tell him to pick you up at 3:15."

Jim said fine, he will meet me right here where he dropped me off.

"Fine," I said.

I wanted to get there an hour before my case was called so I could get my bearings and be familiar with everything before my own case.

I found going thru the metal detector and being wanded lots of fun. To me it is like a game. And the guard told me, "Look on the door outside *Information* to find out where to go."

There was my name, but to my shock it said Judge Karen Smith. I wondered who Judge John was that I had been sharing so much love with in my mind. I felt like I had to start from scratch now.

It said Second Floor Courtroom 9. So I walked up the steps and found Court Room 9. It seemed like a sleepy almost empty room.

There was the girl judge up in front. She had blond hair and looked like a nice woman. The law clerk next to her. And less than a handful of people sitting there.

I was very early and sat at the edge of one bench near the door. And began sending love in my mind to the judge and to everyone there. The clock did not seem to move at all.

Finally she called the first case. A cop sat down on one side, a young man on the other side. The cop said he did not obey the sign. The young man said the sign could not be seen. It had happened at night and he showed pictures to the judge to prove the sign could not be seen.

The judge said "I am going to take these pictures with me and study it for consideration. You will hear tomorrow."

Next came a cop with a lady. He said she had driven thru a stop sign. She said "I was not driving, it was my friend who was driving."

She actually proved this to the judge, and she dismissed her case.

Then the judge said to me "Your Officer is a little late. We are waiting for him."

So I knew the cop was coming and my case would not

be dismissed because no cop showed up. Which is what I had secretly hoped for.

So then the judge left by a door next to the bench. And all that was left in the room was a couple sitting together and the law clerk. And I went back to sending love to the judge and to everyone.

The clock did not seem to move altho two cops arrived and sat in the special area for cops.

I went back to sending love and wondered if that clock would ever move. I looked around and was surprised to see art all over the walls. Framed paintings.

The judge did not reappear. I tried to focus on sending love but it was still almost 2 hours before Jim was supposed to pick me up. I was sure I would get out so early and wondered about a long time waiting for him.

I went back to sending love in my mind to the judge and to everyone in the court room, but it all felt so quiet and sleepy that my eyes started to close over.

I caught myself and began to focus on sending love again when suddenly I jerked fully awake. My own cop had appeared.

I had assumed the man cop, her partner, would be the one, but it was HER! I hadn't realized I hated her till I saw her again for the first time in court. She had been very mean to me in every possible way.

She looked so tall, with such long legs, and without her cap, had very pretty chestnut wavy hair down to her collar.

And she looked nervous. Not like all the other cops. And was in a light grey uniform, not in their dark blue one, and did not look heavily armed as they did. But maybe I didn't see her gun.

As soon as she arrived my praying began in earnest. I now had a real purpose for sending love. I wanted to take away the hate in my mind.

I moved over on the bench so a pillar obstructed my view of her, and her view of me. And I just focused on sending love to her. I did that for quite a while till I was completely harmonious with her in my mind. And then I sent love to her and the judge.

And to my surprise I heard her let out a little cough. She did it two times. I knew what that cough meant. Her mind was responding to all that love.

I was surprised that she was the only one who responded to all the love I had been steadily sending out since I arrived. The judge, the clerk, the cops, the other people who had been waiting for their cases, the couple who still was— no one had responded. Only Officer Jeffries, my arresting officer, responded.

I realized she must be a sensitive girl.

Finally the judge returned. And called my case. We both stood up and raised our right hand and swore to tell the truth, the whole truth and nothing but the truth. Which I fully intended to do and which I did.

Officer Jeffries spoke first. She identified herself. And said she has been on the force since December 2012.

So she had been a cop for just weeks when she stopped me. That explained why she had done such a botched job in every way. She had no experience and no natural talent for the job to boot.

And she is so young, she looked around 23 or 24 the most.

Officer Jeffries testified to the judge that I had been driving nearly a mile in the bike lane and when she stopped me the first thing she asked me was "why was I driving in the bike lane?" And that I had answered "I feel safe driving in the bike lane."

All of this is hooey and never happened.

As I told the judge when it was my turn to talk, "I am learning how to drive. I am now expert at driving around my own residential neighborhood but am just learning how to drive in traffic.

"I had decided to drive to the mini Post Office which is in the residential neighborhood across Speedway Boulevard.

"I waited till there was no traffic coming in the opposite direction, signaled that I was going to turn, but when I looked in my mirror cars were bearing down on me.

"This kept happening, so finally I signaled right, changed lanes and pulled into the bike lane, first looking to see there were no bikes. So I could stop and figure out what I was going to do. All I wanted was to get out of everyone's way.

"However the instant I pulled into the bike lane my friend said 'there is a cop behind you.' I looked in the mirror and sure enough there was.

"I thought the cops would stop me, but instead they kept following me in the bike lane. I had no idea why the cops wanted me to keep driving in the bike lane. Finally they signaled that I should pull over into a driveway behind a building and I did.

"She never asked me why I was in the bike lane. All she said to me is 'license and registration please.' She discovered my learners permit had expired.

"Then I had to sit there for a very long time. And then the man cop got out and gave me two tickets, one for driving in the bike lane, and one for expired license.

"I went down the next day and took the written test all over again and got a new learners permit. Here is my new learners permit. Do you want to see it?"

"No I don't!" the Judge said, "You can show it to the Officer if you like."

I was so surprised.

Jim had told me 100 times to make sure I have my new license with me to show the judge so I would not have to pay that fine. As if I would have forgotten to bring it!

So Officer Jeffries obediently held out her hand to see my new learners permit. Looked at it and handed it back to me. It made no sense to me.

Then the judge asked her about my testimony. And Officer Jeffries said "What she said is exactly what happened."

I was gratified.

So then the judge said I had to pay $195 the fine for driving in the bike lane because I was driving in the bike lane. I said "OK."

Then she said I have to pay the fine for driving without a valid license.

"When do you think you will get your drivers license?" she said to me.

I thought and said "Maybe around same time the monsoons come." (In Tucson that is July 4th.)

She said, "You can come back then and show it to me and you won't have to pay the fine."

I said "Maybe I will just pay the $70 and get it over with. I'll pay both fines now. All I want is to learn how to drive. I don't want to come to court again. How much do both fines come to?"

She said "Driving in the bike lane is 195 and driving without a license is 205."

I said "But I got my new learners permit. I got it the day afterwards."

At that point the judge got very sympathetic but also thought I was a total idiot. She tried every which way to Sunday to explain to me that I needed a drivers license to drive.

I kept trying to say the pamphlet the officer gave me said 70 dollars and I went down the next day and I have my new learners permit.

When she tried to say again I need a drivers license to drive, I interrupted her. I said "I know I need a drivers license to drive. I am not stupid!"

I didn't even try again to find out why it was 205 instead of 70 like the pamphlet said.

By now she was totally sympathetic and on my side just thought she was dealing with a jerk.

She said "I understand you are learning how to drive, maybe you should go to a professional driving school rather than have your friend teach you.

"I'll tell you what I'll do. I'll give you till August 30th to get your license. And if you need more time just call me."

She was such a darling and trying to be so sweet to me. I wanted to say "I love you." Instead I just mouthed the words. I didn't think you were allowed to say "I love you" out loud to a judge at court.

So I went to the clerk so he could do the paperwork for me. He had everything that was especially pertinent blocked out in yellow.

He too like the rest of the court room— Judge Karen, Officer Jeffries, the policemen waiting in the box. And the people who had arrived while my case was going on— all thought I was the biggest idiot in the western world.

But I didn't care. I knew in my heart of hearts it was good for me to have a deadline to get my real drivers license. And the deadline the judge had given me was a good deadline. I actually was in a great mood and loved everyone.

I thought it was a great outcome. I even teased Officer Jeffries as she was standing up in the witness box. "Stay out of my neighborhood!" I said to her. "Stay away from me! If you see me, pretend you don't!"

And I giggled and went down to pay my fine.

I was surprised to see that it was ten after 3. I guess my case had taken a long time.

I was completely merry and happy. It was all over and I thought it was a good outcome. The law clerk had told me to go to the Information Room downstairs to pay my fine.

I asked the girl at the desk "how do I pay my fine?" She gave me a number and said, "it will take one minute for you to be called."

And sure enough after one minute, I was called to Window 17.

I got out my credit card and paid the 195 for driving in the bike lane. And then I giggled to the girl about how I have till August 30th to get my regular license.

I showed her that paper work. I said how the judge said call her if I want more time.

"What is her phone number?"

She said "We don't have it, you'd have to come down here for that."

"It's not worth it to me," I said. "It's more better for me to get my license by August 30th. Can I just show it to you or will I have to show it to the judge?" She said I can show it to her.

I believed her and thought, well then everything is perfect. "Great!" I said.

I was laughing the whole time. I have no idea why I was in such an up mood.

I looked at the clock and it was 3:15 on the dot. I walked out and there was a hot dog man right there. Sitting in one hard chair in the shade with another chair right next to him.

Jim was not there. I was so thirsty and just wanted a cigarette. "Do you have sodas?" I asked.

"Yes," he said.

"What soda do you want?"

He opened up his cooler, all the cans of sodas on ice.

"I wanted a Coke, that seemed perfect after a whole day in court, but I see you have Pepsi. That is fine."

"I have a Coke," he said.

And handed it to me.

"How much?" I said.

"One dollar," he said.

I got out 2 dollar bills. I handed him one for the soda, and another one saying "After a day in court I want luck. This is for you." He was happy to get it.

I looked at the chair right next to him in the shade. "Can I sit here and smoke a cigarette while waiting for my friend to pick me up?"

"Of course," he said.

He was such a nice short Mexican man. Just who you want to see after your afternoon in court.

I was just about to sit comfortably down next to this lovely man, with my soda in my hand and my cigarettes in my purse when Jim drove up.

I got in the car with my unopened can of Coke and sat next to him.

"Well you missed a great show," I said to him. "They all think I am a total idiot. I finally had to tell the judge I'm not stupid and I told Officer Jeffries to stay out of my neighborhood. And I have to get my drivers license by August 30th or pay $205.

"OK" Jim said, "we'll start practicing your tushy turns tomorrow."

"OK" I said.

It took me forever to calm down from my experience.

Altho my Higher Self said, "You did spectacular Anne. You gave love to everyone plus you gave them all a great show."

But when I woke up the next morning all I could think was "How could I have made such an idiot of myself in court!"

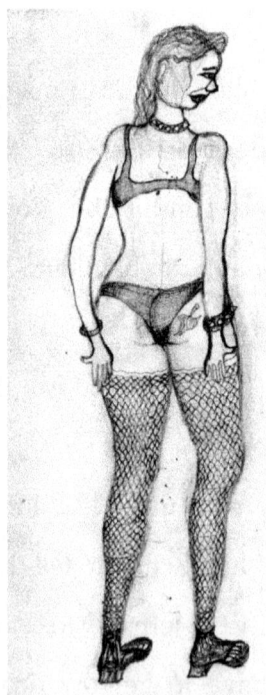

Jim has fantasies about Officer Jeffries. He likes girls with long legs

May 13

Such a sweet driving lesson yesterday

It was Sunday. It was a beautiful day. I didn't want to go all the way up to the DMV and practice my tushy turn there. I know I will have to do it eventually. To pass the test I have to be able to do it in that tight space without even touching any of the cones.

But when you wake up on such a gorgeous morning. And it is a peaceful Sunday. Who wants to be driven for long distance on busy major boulevards past all those big stores and thru mall traffic. All you want is a variation of the peace and beauty you have out your window right now.

Plus the tushy turns are all about passing the road test. I can already do them well enuf for real life. What I really need is practice driving outside my own tiny residential neighborhood where I am usually the only car on the road.

I need real driving practice.

So I decided what I would do instead is drive truck once around my own neighborhood to warm up. Then drive it over to Rosemont and Pima which is a mile on the other side of my neighborhood.

Switch seats with Jim. Have him drive it over to where Glenn Road starts. And then I would drive the truck on that quiet back road all the way to the other end of Tucson and back again to my swim club.

I thought that would give me lots of practice with lights, 4 way stops, driving with other cars on the road. Driving thru major intersections.

So when Jim called at 9:30 I said "it's too pretty a day to go to DMV." I told him my plan instead. I said "my Y pool opens at noon so pick me up at 11."

He was in an up mood when he arrived and so was I. It really was a beautiful day and finally we had both gotten a lot of sleep. We were both well rested.

I got in the drivers side of the truck. Stepped hard on the clutch to switch it to first gear and instantly the truck began slowly rolling. "Fine" I thought, "I'll just steer it out of my driveway."

But when it got to the middle of the street and I kept pressing on the gas nothing happened.

"I must be in the wrong gear" I thought.

And switched gears.

Nothing happened again when I stepped on the gas.

"Am I in first gear?" I asked Jim.

"You're in the right gear" he said.

I stepped harder on the gas. "Maybe because it is a slight hill" I thought.

Nothing happened.

Finally it hit me. I had forgotten to put the key in and turn on the motor.

Instant I did that the car was willing to run. Good thing because I was stretched across Baker Street and finally a car was coming.

"It was because I forgot to put the key in and turn on the motor" I said to Jim.

He couldn't stop laughing. He said "after 2 years of driving lessons, you haven't progressed. You have regressed."

It seemed like an inauspicious beginning to my first real driving lesson since last November, 6 months ago. After being pulled over by Officer Jeffries back in first week of

February, I hadn't been willing to leave my own neighborhood.

But now I was ready to. It was time for me to start driving.

I had already decided that instead of switching seats with Jim at the corner of Rosemont and Pima I would pull into the little driveway behind the building on the corner to switch seats there.

Because that is where the whole drama had taken place. It was in that driveway behind the building that Officer Jeffries had made me pull into. And parked behind me. And major drama had taken place there.

The *Letter From God* for this morning had said *Bless everyone and everything. This is how you turn the earth into golden light.*

So before Jim had even called at 9:30 am I knew I was going to go back to that driveway so I could bless it. So much turmoil had taken place in it.

I didn't tell Jim my plan. He thinks my new age stuff is cuckoo. But he saw me pull to the right as close to the bike lane as I could get (without going in it!) and signaling as I drove slowly along looking for that driveway.

"What are doing!" he said. "This is how you got in

trouble the first time."

I didn't say anything. Turned into that driveway when I saw it and pulled up to where I had been before. But this time I was happy and peaceful and looked around and saw all the pretty trees ahead of me and around me from the yard it was adjacent to.

"We'll change seats here" I said.

"Why!" he said. "You can drive it to Glenn."

But I knew the energy and concentration it would take for me to drive to Glenn and Craycroft would use up my whole mind. I wouldn't be willing to drive on Glenn all the way to other end of Tucson if I did that.

He said "You chose the worst place to change seats!"

So he drove the truck to corner of Craycroft and Glenn for me and pulled up into the church parking lot on Glenn. It was filled with cars. I guess Sunday service was going on.

But I was happy. I had blessed the place where the trauma had happened which took away the booboo that place had given me. And I hadn't used up any of my energy and concentration. Driving there had been a warm-up for me.

So we switched seats in the church parking lot. I remembered to turn the motor on this time, and I pulled into Glenn and began driving.

And I was really driving Glen Road very expertly. All that driving around my own neighborhood did pay off. For the first time I was comfortable switching to third gear and didn't drive the whole way in second. I had the turn signal down pat.

I wasn't relaxed behind the wheel, I was concentrating so hard. And I wouldn't let Jim try to chit chat with me while I was driving. "No talking while I am driving" I said.

And everything was going along fine. I had traveled quite a distance when Jim said "There is cop car in front of you. Don't pull up along side of him."

I never used to be bothered when Jim pointed out a cop car near me. I always thought "a girl learning to drive because her husband went to Heaven, what cop in the world would want to give me a hard time."

That was before Officer Jeffries busted my ass.

Even tho I knew I had not broken any traffic laws, for the first time I noticed I never drive with a seat belt.

I even remembered for the first time that the first thing Officer Jeffries had said to me after "license and registration" and we had gotten it all out for her—

Was "were you driving with seat belt?"

"I don't remember" I said to her.

And she let it pass.

Thank God.

She had too many other things to get me for when she discovered my Learners Permit had expired.

And saw that I was driving barefoot. "You're not allowed to drive barefoot!" she said.

LOL Officer Jeffries, as I found out in court last week, had only been on the force few weeks when she pulled me over. I was the first one she had pulled over. Her partner, the experienced man cop, was there to help her.

I saw the cop car in front of us, my blood ran cold. I don't want to drive anywhere near cops anymore. What if I make a mistake! Plus I realize I am not wearing a seat belt.

Neither Jim nor I ever drive with seat belts.

As soon as I saw the cop all I wanted to do was to pull off Glenn Road into one of the residential neighborhoods and get away from him. I watched carefully so I would not pull into the bike lane and finally made my turn.

I was going to drive around that residential neighborhood at first but to my surprise I discovered I had used up all my concentration. My mind didn't want to work, it wanted to relax.

"Fine" I thought, "I'll switch seats with Jim right now and he can just take me swimming."

It was the first time I had stopped before my mind was completely shot, before I was completely wiped out. I was happy.

I was glad that seeing the cop had stopped my driving. I thought this way I can arrive at the Y with mind and energy intact. And enjoy being there. Enjoy my swim. And still have energy and mind when I return home.

I realized that seeing the cops had done a favor for me. So Jim and I switched seats. And because it was too early for my swim pool to open, for first time in his whole life Jim drove slowly to use up the time.

Which was such a treat for me because for first time I got a chance to look around and see everything, which I really liked.

May 27th

At the Beach

I dream I am at the beach with Bill

I woke up this morning and was looking for something in the saved folder of my email. I don't remember now what it was, maybe the instructions on how to change the batteries in my mouse.

I came across this tiny dream I had written down two months ago. I had forgotten all about it. I didn't remember the dream or that I had written it down. It hadn't seemed important at all at the time. It seemed like such a little dream.

But I read it this morning when I woke up and it interested me. I decided to ask my Higher Self to interpret it for me. And I found what She said very interesting.

Here is the little dream. And after that my Higher Self's interpretation of it this morning.

Dream March 23rd

I dreamt Bill and I were back in Old Forge. I said to Bill "we might as well buy a house here."

At first naturally I wanted one in the countryside but then I realized how nice to be able just to walk to any store you want. So I said "we will get one in town."

Then I went for coffee for both of us. I guess we were on the beach. Because I thought it was a long walk to Rudy's.

So I tried that little snack shop right on the beach.

I thought to myself "here is where it all started" when I first walked in.

Sure enuf they were open, they served coffee.

But I forgot to bring money. I only had nickel and penny.

"I'll be right back" I said to the woman behind the counter.

"Meanwhile make two coffees light and sweet."

But when I went to find Billy I could not find him.

I had said to her "he is on blanket on the beach."

But I guess I entered the wrong part.

I kept calling his name loud, hoping he would answer.

Interpretation by my Higher Self

I take down Her words as she says them to me

Anne had this dream a week after her second year without Bill had started. She was scared when she saw on the calendar that the anniversary of his "change of address" was a week away. She thought "Is it going to be emotional and intense for me. Will I cry."

She hadn't cried at the time it happened. Because I had lifted her up to a place so happy and high and love filled that tears were out of the question, sadness was out of the question.

There was only the great adventure of a brand new life starting this instant.

But of course some tears came later. Usually in the evening. When she was lying in her backyard under the stars.

She knew he was perfectly happy, happier than he had ever been, she knew it was just a change of address. And they were in constant communication. His love for her was constant and increased.

She was never away from his love but it seemed unbearable he wasn't in the house with her. She did not want to be unhappy and I did not want her to be unhappy. So it only lasted a moment, that sob under the stars at night. That first week.

Instantly she would turn to me to be lifted up back into happiness again. Which I was able to do by tenderly and lovingly explaining everything to her. It was usually an hour. It was a long talk.

It began off with an instant of suspense because Anne could see no way she could be lifted from such depth of unhappiness to high and happy place.

But there is nothing I cannot do.

For me it is easy as pie. In less than an instant I had her drinking in my love and listening eagerly to my explanation. And by the time it was over she was higher and happier than she had ever been. And at perfect peace.

No one believed Anne when she told them she never lost her happiness when she lost Bill. But she was telling them the truth.

She had found the way to hold onto her happiness. And I was the way.

But of course two years later with her happiness assured— it had been two years of happiness, she was so secure about her happiness, and so relaxed into it— she assumed she would be open to any sadness which came her way on the two year anniversary.

It never occurred to her there would be no sadness at all. But that is exactly what happened. None came to her.

And this is the dream she had before she woke up a week later.

Old Forge in Anne's dreams is the emblem of paradise. It is where she spent her childhood summers and her experience of them had been paradise.

The dream opens up with her and Bill in Old Forge together. The first thing she says is "let's buy a house here." Meaning let's make our home here. She assumes she wants one in the midst of beautiful nature.

Bu then she is practical. She realizes she will want to

walk to everything, so she switches and says "we'll get a house in town instead."

This is OK. It's a more balanced choice. After all it's a tiny town, just a hamlet in the Adirondack mountains. The little hamlet is in the midst of beautiful wilderness.

She wants both, the beautiful forest and a lovely happy easy life filled with treats in the midst of it. Living in town is good idea. It means she has envisioned her life there. She is planning to settle down there.

They are on the town beach when this conversation takes place. The beach by the lake where Anne spent every year of her childhood summers. She knows that beach and that lake by heart.

She is one with that beach, with that lake too. The water of that lake and the sand of that beach.

The beach has a little snack bar right on it. When she was a kid it had a pinball machine and the teenagers were always at the pinball machine. And a counter where they sold food. And a juke box.

It is where Anne heard *Rock Around the Clock* for the first time. She heard rock and roll for the first time in that snack bar. And Elvis Presley too she heard for the first time there, *Heartbreak Hotel.*

Because of the pinball machine, the teenagers, and the juke box, it was always the emblem of the teenage world for Anne. A world of beautiful gods and goddesses, who do what gods and goddesses do. Play pinball, look beautiful, listen to the jukebox. And do teenage things.

Her one dream as a child was to be a teenager. And be a goddess herself and hang out with the other gods and goddesses and have all the fun that gods and goddesses have.

She never sat at that counter or bought anything at that counter. She only went in to play pinball with her cousin Richie.

The beach had another snack bar, much smaller, further up the rocks. She never bought anything there either but she once watched in fascination as the girl made a grilled cheese sandwich for someone on the grill. It looked so delicious to Anne. And she never forgot all the steps the girl did.

And when she moved to Tucson she would make grilled cheese sandwiches exactly that way.

But if you walked past that other snack bar which was on a hill. Continue walking up the hill over the rocks you came to Rudy's. And this is where Anne did spend a lot of time and bought things.

Every afternoon she went there for her ice cream cone. And then went back to get an ice cream cone for her mom.

And when the beach closed, the lifeguards went home and the tourists left, she and Richie looked around and under all the benches at the back of the beach, and in all the trash cans, to find bottles to return to Rudy's for two cents. And Anne bought comic books and candy bars with her share of the money at Rudy's.

She loved Rudy's, it had everything a child wanted.

In the dream she is all grown up and wants a container of coffee for her and Bill. She wonders if the beach snack bar sells coffee, she has no idea, or if she will have to make the trek over the rocks to Rudy's for it.

But to her happy surprise the beach snack bar does have it.

She walks in, she is back in it, everything is the same as it was, and her first thought is "this is where it all began." She means her life and her dreams.

But she forgot to bring money with her. She sees she only has nickel and penny. She has to go back to her husband to get the money. She says "He is on the blanket. I'll be back right away. Meanwhile make us the coffee, two containers light and sweet."

But she can't find him. She realizes she entered a different part of the beach. She calls his name loudly, so he can wave her over to him. But the dream ends with her calling his name loudly.

She has lost Bill. The snack bar stands for the world. After all, her whole experience as a child was the lake and the beach.

The snack bar was for teenagers. It was a teenage hang out. It stood for everything the world has to offer, but you have to be a teenager to have it. In fact being a teenager is what the world offers.

Anne couldn't wait to be a teenager and have all that too. LOL she thought quintessential paradise was the future. She had stars in her eyes all the time about the future. Her glorious future.

And while it is true when you did enter that paradise of being a teenager, you can never find your way back to the pure happiness you had as a child. The world and being a teenager turned out not to be fun at all, happiness is the happiness you had. It doesn't get better than that.

So Anne walks in and thinks "this is where it all began." Meaning this is where I first dreamed of the world and wanted so much to be in it.

Obviously in the dream, altho she is not aware of it, she and Bill are hanging out in Heaven together. She plans to settle down with him there. "We'll buy a house here" she says.

She goes to get them coffee. Light and sweet.

But she enters the world and can't find him again. Because he is not in the world.

Poor little Anne. She doesn't realize this. And thinks by calling his name loudly, he will hear her and call her over. But that's not the way it works. She won't find him in the world. Because they weren't in the world.

Darling the world is one place in your mind, Heaven is another. Honeybunch you were just looking in the wrong part of your mind for him. Of course you will be back with Bill. It's impossible he be taken from you.

But honeybunch you will have to find the place in your mind where he is and you are too, and where you are always together, to be back with him.

And eventually you will find that place. Even if you haven't found it yet.

I love you

Your Higher Self

How it all began

I never thought I would reveal all this but my Higher
Self talked me into it...

How She talked me into it

I take down Her words as She says them to me

Anne's novel of her first 6 months of this year is written.
Now is time to edit it. She is not having an easy time with
the editing. She doesn't know what to leave in and what to

take out. She doesn't know if she should introduce certain parts, or just leave them as is.

And she wants to add Bill's cartoons. The ones which were all in a folder she has already used in her previous books. She doesn't even know where to begin to look to find other ones.

LOL so the whole process of editing the book. She had loved writing it but editing is turning into a headache for her. Each day for past week she sits down and starts, but after an hour she can't take it and runs away.

LOL the more she runs away, the more it builds up in her mind that it is a very hard thing to do and that she doesn't want to do it and she will never be able to succeed in it.

But of course she has no choice. She wants to publish her book. And the only way is to edit it. She has to turn what she wrote over the 6 months into a book.

She is going to have to face doing everything she doesn't want to do now. She has to find a way to do it. And she will.

The first step in editing is reading your whole book thru from beginning to end. You have to find out what is in there.

Because editing is all decision making. And editing a novel (unlike editing a short story or a chapter) is making decisions based on the book as a whole.

You have to have some picture of your book as a whole to base your decisions on.

And because Anne writes her novels day by day as her life unfolds, she does not have the slightest idea of what is in there till she finishes writing it and has to read it thru from beginning to end as the first step in editing.

This is always the hardest part for Anne because her resistance is highest. For her it is always the same as going off the first time that super high diving board in the Aquacade in Queens near where Anne grew up.

The Aquacade was built for the World's Fair before Anne was born. A huge pool with stadium like seating all around it. And diving boards of various heights. And one is incredibly high.

And Anne was 11 years old and used to the little diving board on the lake in the Adirondacks where she swam every summer. She had taught herself how to do a swan dive off of that.

But this was built for divers to do so many somersaults in the air before they reached the water.

For top notch divers. But of course Anne wanted to do her little swan dive off of that. It seemed so much more exciting than little swan dive off a diving board not that far from the water.

She would get on line to climb all those steps to reach it. And when it was her turn she would walk to end of the diving board and look down.

And it was such a far distance down, she would get scared, walk back from the edge of the diving board and climb all the steps back down again.

She would do this 3 times and then force herself to go off the board. And after that she wasn't scared to do it. She knew what the experience was like.

She had the identical experience when she began writing for the first time. Because she didn't know if she would be able to do it. But this time there was no turning back. She was at the edge of the diving board, she knew she had to take the plunge. And she did.

And after that she never had that experience with writing again until it came to editing her previous two novels and this one too.

Altho with her previous two novels when she reached the edge of the diving board and had to take the plunge she just did. And to her happy surprise when she discovered what she had written, she liked it. So that problem was easily solved. The rest is all the hard decision making.

But with this new novel, it was worse than the first time at the high diving board at the Aquacade. It wasn't fear, it was sheer resistance. It took her 5 tries to even reach the edge of the diving board. She simply turned around and went back.

Then when she forced herself to make the plunge she got exactly nowhere. Instead of the resistance disappearing as she began to read it, the resistance increased.

All five times she gave up after the first ten pages. And then she didn't want to go back to it at all.

But today is July 4th. Her pool is closed, altho Jim's pool is open. I suggested she give Jim the whole day off. Skip the driving lesson.

Let him go to his club at the time he actually likes to go and stay as long as he wants, talk to his friends. Have a whole day off to suit himself. Have zero responsibility for Anne.

Anne said to me "What will I do with myself, a whole long day at home?"

"Let's go back to trying to read your novel thru," I

suggested. "We'll do it differently this time. We'll begin at the end and work our way forwards."

Anne was game so we did it.

A very interesting thing happened to her when she got to the part in book where she told the girls who had been in her womens lib group how she bought Irene's painting back in NYC a month before her New York City life collapsed and she moved to Tucson.

It had actually been 6 months prior to telling them this— It was Thanksgiving weekend when the girls in this little group, this little email group, began letting down their hair with each other.

It all began when Fran mentioned about having been in AA.

These were girls who had not seen each other since they had all been in their early twenties back in the 1960s. They were all such young sparkly happy girls filled with idealism, doing what came naturally to them. Making a revolution and having a ball doing it.

Never had they expected to confide about the hell which came into their life in 1983 and became almost a constant companion for next 25 years, altho the girls got better and better at handling it.

And for each girl it had been their spiritual path. Each fresh bout of hell advanced them on their path. LOL these were girls who were tremendously motivated to learn.

Hahaha there is nothing like suffering to motivate you. You will do anything to get out of suffering.

And even tho all these girls had been atheists during the days when they were in womens liberation. Hadn't Karl Marx said "religion is the opiate of the masses."

LOL and they were idealists, intellectuals, revolutionaries, and New Yorkers. Adventurous girls with a great sense of fun and adventure. Wild pot smoking hippies too.

Giggle giggle life sees to it that you fulfill your destiny. You do fulfill everything you signed up for before you arrive on Earth. You don't want to but you do.

You are brought kicking and screaming to the place where you have no choice but to fulfill the assignment you chose to undertake before you arrived.

They were the Sixties generation. And they were chosen, hand picked if you like, this whole generation was hand picked, to help the world rise into love.

Quite simply to choose love instead of fear.

In truth Anne only knows her own odyssey. Yes she had

once read a book by a man just her age who went thru his odyssey at exactly the same time as Anne did.

The worst of their odyssey, those first 4 years, when everything happens, and all the big changes are made. The real learning the real growth. After that you are tempered steel. You have learned unconditional love.

You have chosen love instead of fear.

All you are meant to do is to love everyone.

You have chosen love.

Anne's generation fulfilled its mission. The ascent of the planet into love was now guaranteed.

When her life collapsed totally in the Autumn of 1991 I told Anne to move to Tucson. And a month later she and Bill and their dog Clio walked into their new Tucson apartment.

It is interesting that that final week while Bill was packing up everything in the NYC apartment for their move and carting it in a hand truck to the post office, Anne's dreams at night were all about graduation.

In every dream she was handed a diploma she was told "you graduated," she had graduated high school.

Altho in one dream her old high school, Jamaica High School, was a law school instead, which is very interesting.

Because isn't that what God's law is. God's law is love. For God law and love are the same thing.

Anne had graduated into love.

For most their education stops here. That is all that is asked of anybody, it is what is asked of everybody, to graduate into love.

To move into love.

But it turns out a few souls had signed up for post graduate studies. And it turns out that unbeknownst to Anne, her soul was one of those who did.

She did continue to have difficulties in Tucson, but let's not talk about that now. The purpose of them was simply to help Anne reach a higher understanding. Which she did.

She reaped great benefits from these travails. And even tho she is still pissed off at Me for what I put her thru, all the cards aren't in yet, Anne may come to see it all differently.

But if she confided to these 5 girls who were in her womens lib group back then the very first steps on her path— just because she never told anyone else, and never expected to tell anyone, why not put these few emails in her book now.

Everyone has been on an odyssey of sorts, some may

recognize their own experience in them. And some may find it interesting reading someone else's experience.

So I am asking Anne to include them here now even tho they don't appear to be part of this book at all. They are not her new life right now. But they are what started it all off.

The purpose of this book is not for Anne to write a good book, the one single purpose of this book is that if there is anything in her experience which can in any way help another, that is my one single purpose for Anne's book.

LOL what is the purpose of putting Anne thru the mill, if not because it would benefit her and others....

(from Anne) OK I will do it. Here are the 4 emails I wrote my little group back in November. The first is intense, the others are lighter and sweeter

How it all began

It all began when I hit bottom, I had to find a solution

November 29, 2012

Jean, your whole long honest depthful email to us here is priceless to me. And being on this thread with you girls is priceless to me.

I don't think I would have ever understood my life without it.

First of all I never knew there was a name for my life changing experience. I knew I had hit bottom. I knew I had lost all. I knew that all I wanted in the whole world was to recover what I had lost. That it was priceless to me.

But I was alone in my experience because I had lost it all from letting my emotions control me. I knew I had to give up anger and fighting. I had lost everything because of my anger and my fighting.

To get my husband back I had to regain his trust, which I had destroyed. And to get this back I had to be gentle and kind with perfect consistency. I had to be loving, and nothing but loving.

I knew I had to stop fighting to save my life. I had so exhausted and depleted myself from fighting, every night for several years, that I could not even go to work. I wondered if I was going to physically survive, there was no energy left at all.

I was wrecked physically, mentally, emotionally.

This is what my fighting had done to me.

My first idea was to ask him can we stop fighting. I thought in order for it to happen he had to agree with it. But I knew he would not agree to it, because he would not agree with me on anything at that point.

And then I made my first important insight. "It takes two to make a fight and if I don't fight back there is no fight." Eureka! It meant I could stop the fighting all on my own and I did not need him to agree with it.

That evening after he got home from work and we were watching a little tv he began a fight. Who began all the fights over the previous 3 years I do not know? But of course this time I noticed. I guess he said awful things to me or began berating me.

I kept my mouth shut. I knew attacking back is how I would start fighting and I didn't want to fight.

Probably those first things he said weren't that bad, he was used to me attacking at this point.

So he increased it. I still kept my mouth shut. I did not

want to fight. I was determined to save my life and the only way was to stop fighting.

So he pulled out all the stops. He let loose saying awful things to me.

And that is when I heard that awful shrieking voice (I guess it was my ego) ordering me to attack.

"ATTACK!!" it ordered. "Are you a man or a mouse! Are you going to take this lying down! **ATTACK!! ATTACK NOW!!**"

It was probably the most suspenseful moment of my whole life. I actually watched every fiber of my being, every part of my mind, instantly obey the order, line up for attack. The words I would say to attack actually rose all the way to my mouth to my very lips.

I considered for an instant reversing my decision, decided not to.

The attack words were still at the door of my lips wanting to burst out. All of me wanted to burst out in attack. But I did not want to. I wanted to hold my decision not to fight.

I did not know what was going to happen.

I watched in total suspense.

And I saw the words could not burst out. They could

rise all the way to my lips but go no further. A whole army was at my lips raring to go, but could not go. My decision not to fight held them in check. They had to recede.

I settled down.

So then he did it again. It was worse than before. He didn't begin off pussyfooting around this time, he just went straight to it worse than before.

Again I heard the order to attack. Again I heard that voice (I guess it is the first time I heard the ego as something other than myself, before that I always thought the ego was myself) ordering me to attack. Taunting me "Are you a man or a mouse! You can't take this lying down!"

This time when I reconsidered my decision, I actually considered. I was tempted. But then I realized if I were to attack back now, that everything I had just accomplished with such momentous effort would go to naught. I would have undone it.

I decided to stick with my decision. So I watched the whole process take place again. The whole army rushed to obey the ego's order to attack. Altho of course then I knew nothing about ego. It was just a voice in my mind that for the first time I did not think was me.

Again I watched in suspense to see if it would burst thru my lips. Again I saw it did not, it seemed as if it *could* not. As tho I would have to reverse my decision for it to do it. I didn't reverse my decision. It stayed at my very lips chomping at the bit. And then again it had to go back, all the way back.

I WON!!

WHEW I had made it.

It may have happened 4 times that evening. It was what happened instead of the fight we had every night.

The process always repeated itself but gradually the suspense wasn't as intense. I knew now it could not get thru my lips unless I reversed my decision. And I was never tempted to reverse my decision again. I knew I was succeeding in my goal not to fight.

When it was all over he had exhausted himself berating me, he had nothing else to say. I had not said one word all thru it. I hadn't added any fuel to the fire.

I realized I had to communicate to him that I was not mad at him, or he would think he had to start up again.

I said "I'm going to the kitchen, can I get you anything, would you like a juice or a beer." Of course he wanted a beer. All I wanted was an excuse to show love. I wanted to show love so he would know I am not mad at him. "I am happy to get you a beer" I said. And came back and handed it to him with love.

We got into bed to go to sleep. And I lay there and realized for the first time in my whole life I was proud of myself.

I had done something I never thought I could do in a million years. I had done something I thought I was incapable of doing.

I remember feeling like I was ten feet tall. I had grown from a midget to ten feet tall in my own mind. For the first time I had stature in my own mind.

And for the first time in 3 years I slept like a baby, instead of tossing and turning all night so upset from the fight.

This same scenario repeated itself each night for the summer. But each night I got better at it. I discovered it was easier for me if I did not hear his words berating me. I didn't know how to shut out his words. I tried to say the words to the Star Spangled Banner to myself to shut out his words.

But I never had to deal with the attack army or the ego shrieking at me to attack. I really don't remember much about it after that first night when it happened 4 times.

It became simply an ordeal. And each time when he finished I was careful to say something loving, to go to the kitchen and offer him anything he wanted.

I knew there was nothing he wanted, I just wanted to offer and speak lovingly. And each night I slept like a baby.

And then it stopped happening. He stopped wanting to have a fight with me when he got home from work. He stopped being so angry with me. We just watched tv peacefully together, and talked friendly and nice with each other.

I was always loving to him. I really wanted to get his trust back.

I remember he began to paint the apartment. He was doing all the work, I was just showing appreciation. He was so happy. He said "You know what I just noticed, we haven't had a fight in a long time." He looked so pleased with himself.

"Wow you're right" I said to him.

And to myself I said "I wonder why!!!"

And I would say all of my spirituality began with that. My decision not to fight.

Love Annie

My next email to them written that same afternoon

O Leslie thank you for this wonderful email.

Boxcar Ted was your angel, he is the one who saved you.

For you it was Boxcar Ted, for me it was Tommy Masciotta. Whose wife had kicked him out, and he spent all day every day sitting morosely on my stoop. And the nights sleeping in the abandoned lot next door.

What Tommy Masciotta said to me when I was still fighting with Bill and everything was so awful. I had rushed out of the house late at night I was so upset. Tommy was sitting on the stoop.

I said to Tommy "I've had it! I can't take anymore! I'm moving to Jackson Heights."

He said "Bill really loves you Anne."

It was the words I needed to hear most in the whole world. It calmed me down. I sat down next to him.

He said "Let me buy you a container of coffee."

I said "I have coffee upstairs."

He said "It's not the same, how do you like it, light and

sweet?"

"Yes" I said "thank you."

"What would you like with it? How about a bagel and cream cheese."

"I don't know" I said, "I'm too upset to eat."

"Come on" he said, "a bagel and cream cheese is nice."

"OK" I said, "we can share it."

He said "I can't eat it I have no teeth."

"O" I said. "OK" I said "I'll have bagel and cream cheese. Please get something for yourself too."

The store was right on the corner. We sat there companionably, drank our coffee and ate our nosh. And then all calmed down I went back upstairs.

It was the worst time in Tommy's life, it was the worst time in mine. I guess saving me is how Tommy saved himself

Love, Annie

Another email an hour later

Thank you Jean for your beautiful loving words. Also for your truth. I am interested in this line from your lovely loving email. *We are all on this path together. Isn't that amazing (grace)?*

Half of our thread seems to be sharing our experiences with each other. The other half is our joy and astonishment that we are all here together now sharing these experiences.

I did have brief companionship at the start of my path. It was your own very dear friend Irene. We were on the same path and every evening reported to each other and discussed our experiences of that day and the day before. And learned together.

We helped each other in the beginning. Which were the hardest parts. We assisted each other.

She dropped out in 1987, so maybe it was just that first crucial year. After that I continued climbing alone. Altho of course Heaven sent great angels to help me as soon as I was alone. In my case it was the homeless men on the Lower

East Side.

I would sit on the bench with them while I was walking my dog. Or on the stoop. I never could have made it without their constant love, understanding, encouragement.

As you know my path was saving my marriage.

And what is so interesting Jean, is that all of the men I was friends with had been in long term marriages like mine. They dearly dearly dearly loved their wife. And their wife had thrown them out for the drinking and acting up.

When I was friends with them (1987 till end of 1991 when I moved to Tucson) none of them were willing to have a home without their wife. They were all living on the street.

It was so helpful to me to be with men who loved their wife that much. By their example and their encouragement I was always able to believe Bill loved me.

Also their stories of their shenanigans which got them thrown out, took the edge off the shenanigans I was experiencing too. They were all variations of the same shenanigans.

Also getting to know their noble loving warm hearts and their wisdom.

In some ways they were my closest friends during those 4 years because I didn't have to keep up appearances for them, and they had no appearance to keep up for me.

We met heart to heart.

I was saved by the homeless men in New York City.

From them and from my own experience I gained a depth of understanding which never left me.

Love and kisses, Annie

An hour later I wrote them this one

Hi Pat

Thank you for this email. I really did have a wonderful time with the homeless men during those last 4 years before I left NYC for Tucson when my life was the hardest it ever was in my whole life.

When I was going thru my ordeals (and they were so long lasting back then, and one followed on the heels of another so soon) their love and understanding saved me. The nobility of their being.

As if they all came from such a high place. I think they were all close to God too. Just as I was. We shared that, the reality and love of God.

Thinking of it now I realize our heads were in the same place. I did not have this with anyone else then.

And when things were fine for me (in between ordeals) I had such a good time with the homeless.

They were all selling used clothes on the sidewalk. (The girls in New York leave their used clothes on top of the garbage can in front of their building for anyone to help themself. The homeless find them, fold them up nicely, lay them on the sidewalk and sell them for 50 cents or a dollar.)

I was walking my dog. All the clothes I bought back then was from them. I would stop on the way with my doggie and look at all their clothes on the sidewalk. Pick out a dress, hold it up, and say "where is your fitting room?"

I don't think they ever got my jokes. So then I would hold it up and say "Do you like it? Will it look good on me?"

They would study for a while and give me their opinion. If they said they liked it and it would look good on me I bought it. I would say "How much is it?"

Whatever they said, I said "That is too low." I would give them double what they asked for.

It was such a joyous way of doing business.

There was one young man on Second Avenue between 5th and 6th Streets. I got a really cute skirt from him, lots of ruffles just what I like. The label inside said Clio, that was the name of my dog.

Each time I saw him I would hail him, "My couturier!" I would say

I don't think he knew what a couturier is. I don't think even my husband knows. It is in-joke for girls.

"My couturier!" I would say. "Do you have anything cute for me today?"

He would say "My mother is mad at me." And he would tell me why his mother was mad at him.

There was an old lady, Mary, who sold old clothes on the sidewalk right in front of my building. The homeless men would help her. I bought a dress from her and a winter jacket my last morning before leaving for Tucson, it was mid November.

I told them all "We are moving to Tucson tomorrow."

I hadn't told any of my friends. One of the men said he had been there.

"What is it like?" I asked him. I was so curious.

"There are not many trees" he said.

Turned out the Tucson winter is so mild I wore that little winter jacket every night when the night turned cold.

And a month later when Bill's family came to visit us from San Diego and stayed with in-laws in Tucson, I wore the dress I had bought from Mary on the sidewalk to the Christmas dinner. It was black jersey with an L in rhinestones.

I guess Bill's mom assumed I got the dress at JC Penney. She said "What a nice dress, what does the L stand for?"

I was so flummoxed. When you buy old clothes from the homeless on the street it never occurs to you the letter in rhinestones is 'sposed to be your initial.

I am really glad Bill's family came to visit us in Tucson. I had never met them before. They were wonderful to me and I loved them.

Bill's dad was fun. As soon as Bill and I arrived for Christmas in the afternoon, Loretta, the in-law, served food to me and Bill, his dad, and Bill's 18 year old nephew.

To my surprise Bill's dad broke into song at the table. He sang some popular song from World War 2.

So I sang Al Robinson's favorite song

My gal's a corker

She's a New Yorker

She's got a pair of hips

Just like a battleship.

Bill's dad and his nephew thought I was lotsa fun.

Bill of course was totally embarrassed.

LOL he wanted to look good in front of his dad, you know impress your father...

Love Annie (PS Al Robinson was a boyfriend of Ruthie's, I learned that song from him, it sure came in handy when I met Bill's dad for the first time LOL LOL LOL.

Happy Summer

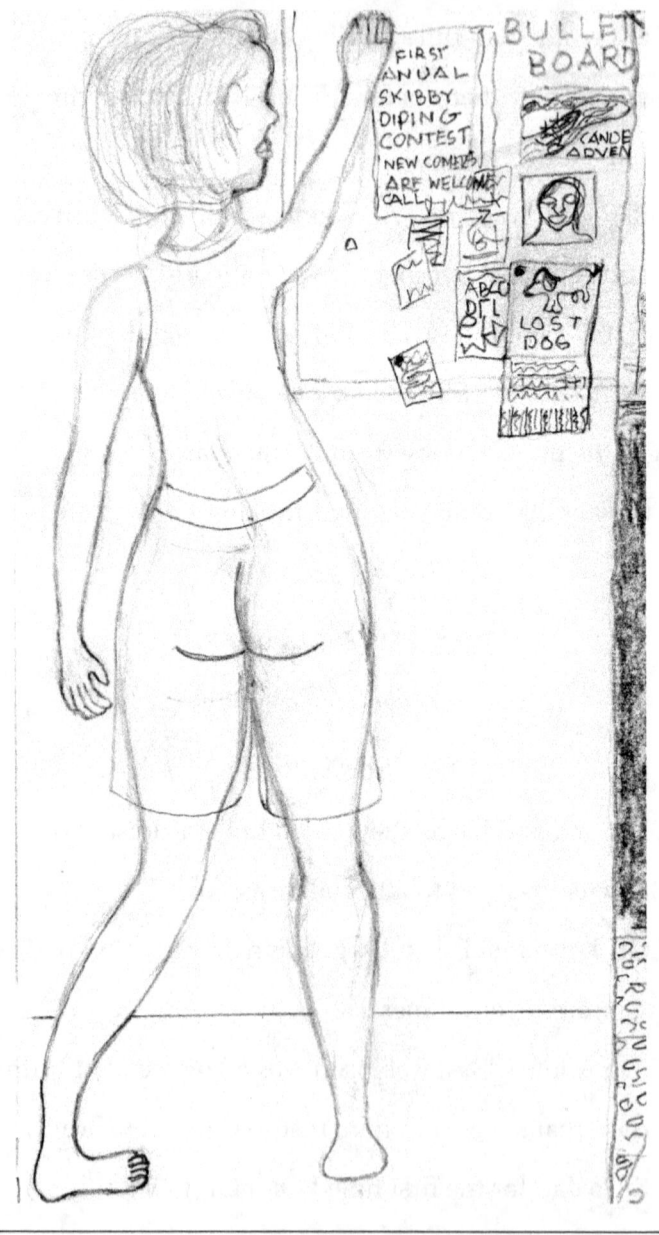

May 22 very early morning

Dawn on the desert

Summer on the desert has arrived. The loveliness of this early morning time is pure joy. It is oddly simple. Just the call of the morning dove filling the air, that deep penetrating call. Some faint twittering coming from nests.

And this amazing light. Who can describe 5:30 in the morning summer desert light. It is a pearl light but not milky like a pearl. The color of pearl but crystal clarity.

I know what it is like! It is as if you were looking thru a lens of something and suddenly it came into perfect focus.

You hadn't realized it was slightly blurry, slightly off, till suddenly it is perfect focus. And it takes your breath away. Because the sublime beauty is in the perfect focus. It makes everything you look at beautiful.

The way you can see the detail. The curlicue leaf on the desert tree right out my window I see is made up of tiny green horizontals with space between each one.

Not only do I see all the little horizontals but I see the minute space between each one. The air shows thru it. They are almost like see-thru leaves. No wonder they can take the great heat of our summer. Most of the leaf is air. Air blows thru every part of it.

LOL it is like a leaf in a string bikini. Hardly anything is covered up. They can take the great heat of our summer because the leaves are all dressed in their string bikinis. The air blows around them and thru them at the same time.

The golden light of the sun is coming in now. Turning the leaves green. My backyard is no longer the pearl color of dawn, that grayish pearl.

The tree out my window has turned a luminescent green. It is lit up from a ray of the sun. In the back of yard it is still shade, the leaves are all dark green now. LOL forest green. But they too will turn chartreuse when the sun's light reaches them.

I bet the trees and their leaves love bathing in the sun's light when it is the gentle light of early morning. The light is gentle and golden and air is still so cool.

I do not know how any living being can withstand the heat and brightness of our summer afternoons. But the trees are just like me delighting in this early morning loveliness, lovely in every way.

Not only the trees and their leaves but the huge pigeons in my backyard. Even my so very naughty cat, Cupcake. Hiding in the tall grass around the tree eying them intently. It is so suspenseful when Cupcake is in the yard, not moving a muscle patiently intently watching them. I know she is up to no good.

O my darling birds. No wonder only the huge pigeons come into my yard now. Who would ever want to come into a yard where Cupcake is out to get you.

O she finally got up and is walking across the yard. She walks like a tiger in the jungle. O she headed into that cactus underbrush on the side of the yard. I think she thinks she will have better luck finding small birds in that area.

Nothing about Cupcake is normal. On one hand she is the biggest scaredy cat in the western world, she won't even let me pet her.

Which makes no sense. She was born right here. She still lives with her mother. Other than being taken to the vet to be fixed after she had her first litter of kittens, all she has had is life on a silk cushion. It has been a peaches and cream life.

I wait on her hand and foot. But the closest she will come to me is to sit on my windowsill sometimes while I sleep.

Sometimes she will let me sneak in one pet when she is eating her kitty treats. She loves her kitty treats. And each time I get up she races to the table so I will pour out some more of them for her.

But she has those wild eyes. I notice them when I am passing on the patio from my bedroom to the kitchen and she is lounging in the hot afternoon in the shady spot of my patio on top of the washing machine. She looks up when I pass and I see her wild eyes.

She is always wary.

O here comes a sweet young morning dove. He is hopping up my tree. They hop from branch to branch. And then fly off.

Well morning has started. It is no longer dawn's early light out there. It is no longer perfect quiet and that sweet hush. I can hear the city starting up in the distance.

O NO! I saw bird feathers on the floor near the table in other room. Killer Cupcake has been up to it again.

I knew last evening when I passed by that table and I

saw her crouched in the corner watching me with such secretive look on her face. As if she were hiding something and didn't want me to take it away.

You don't realize how expressive cat's faces are till you live with them. Everything which is going on shows all over their face.

JUNE

Quelle beauty! Today is so pretty the blue sky is tinged with violet. It is the prettiest day I have ever seen. The crystal clarity of the light turns it into a day in paradise. And there is a light happy vibe to go with it

My FaceBook post June 5th

June on the Desert

Swim pool lassie

June is here in its full summer glory. Desert summer glory is not the lush green summer world everywhere else. Nothing at all grows on the desert in summer. The plant world has to wait for the monsoons which arrive on July 4th to be watered.

Summer glory on the desert which takes place in June is

all about heat and light. It is the month of our beauty, heat, and light climaxing. A month of crystal clarity, color, blue skies the green of desert trees.

Enchanted loveliness of morning and evening. And afternoons of unfathomable heat and brightness. Everything about June on the desert is a trip. It's the apotheosis of everything, the beauty, the clarity, the light, the heat.

And as soon as the month is over the monsoons arrive. Lightning thunder and blessed rain.

That is our July and August.

For me happy summer is June. Altho by the time June is over we become one being awaiting our rains. That is when rock and tree, earth and animal, human and bird and insect, the animal vegetable mineral world and human world too, we become one mind, one heart, all we want most in world is rain.

We are waiting for that crack of thunder so loud it could be heard from here to Canarsie. And that lightning so intense it turns red and takes up the whole sky. To announce they are bringing us our rain. We live on this rain all year. LOL this is how the desert gets watered.

The fanfare of its arrival is a not to be believed show.

There is no thunder like it, there is no lightning like it. It goes on for hours and hours every day for 6 weeks and climaxes and releases itself in rain.

This is our future once glorious June starts. June is the idyllic summer paradise, that deep peace, the depths of quiet, before the wild raging drama which takes over our sky and desert for two months. When we get the show of shows and life giving rain is brought to the desert.

Is it any wonder I love living here.

We who do live here and love it can easily understand why no one else would.

After all during our glorious summer month June you cannot step one foot outside the house in the afternoon.

Even the lizards and snakes who find the world too cold to reside in so they sleep in the earth all winter and don't come out till it is 90 degrees, they can't take our June afternoons either.

They find shady spots to doze all afternoon. The shade is 10 degrees cooler than out in the sun. It makes a difference. A huge difference. Because after you hit 100 degrees, each degree above that feels like 10 degrees. It is an exponential difference in the experience of the heat.

So being in the shade makes it comfortable to be outside,

it is the only way to be comfortable outside for man or beast, bird or insect.

The heat itself increases continuously all afternoon till it finally climaxes at 4 pm.

That is the point when you can't stand it anymore. By that point even having both coolers in your house turned up to high are beaten by the heat. The heat has won.

All you can do is wait for sunset, when the whole huge heat goes bye-bye. Fortunately on the desert sunset comes early.

And as soon as it does lovely life starts up again. Afternoon heat is the intermission in your day.

You can't do anything, you can't think anything. No one can take a 4 hour siesta. For an hour you watch tv. Sleep overcomes you during the show. You wake up an hour later. It is mid afternoon you come to your desk.

Spaced out from sleep and dreams you think your mind will click on. But it doesn't. You try everything to interest you on the computer. At 4 pm you want to give up. You are hot and dazed. You are in a worse stupor than when you arose from siesta. And frustrated too.

You are about to give it all up. "I'll just water the house plants" you think, "and then go back to lounging on the bed. Maybe the TV will have something interesting."

But by that time it is 5 o'clock and life returns to the desert. The birds arrive in the backyard, shadows in your yard begin. Energy rises again, all the energy which you thought was nada, which didn't exist, comes back. What a life! 5 o'clock the return of the energy.

So after you water your house plants and think "I'll give it one more college try at the computer," for some reason it all catches.

FaceBook becomes interesting again. You are able to write a comment. You are able to edit one of your stories instead of blankly staring at it. If it is a week day you might even get an email.

I guess that is June on the desert. Life in the morning, life in the evening, and a long blank afternoon.

No wonder I think "how can anyone but a loony tune like me love this world of June on the desert."

June 7th mid afternoon

Serious heat is here

Serious heat is here. Climbing above 100 degrees is one thing. Climbing above 105 degrees is something else. Yesterday 106, today 109.

It's an entirely different world, a different head. The whole experience of life changes. It's a season unto itself, the season of serious heat.

There is something oddly pleasant about having a mind be blitzed. The heat completely relaxes you and totally shuts off your mind. Activity is out of the question.

You flop on the bed and watch shows you never watched before. You are a happy idiot, easy to please.

O a breeze has started! One of our June breezes has started. Shaking the treetops. That's oddly reassuring too. Wind means motion, it means the air is in motion.

And when you are looking out at a world which is 109

degrees out there, you need to see some evidence of motion, you need to see motion itself, to be reassured life is still going on.

LOL the heat beat everything but it can't beat the wind. The great heat can stop everything, bring everything to standstill, except the wind. The wind follows its own laws and blows when it wants to.

Maybe that is why it is so reassuring to see it blow the tree tops out my open window.

I appreciate there is a sign that the heat is not supreme. Giggle giggle of course it is blowing the hot air from outside all over me. But so what! I am just so glad to see something in motion. I want to remember the world is still alive.

Post script 4 hours later at 7:30 pm

I made it thru the afternoon. It is just after sunset now. The insane heat is byebye, it leaves with the sun. The yard is in shadow which is so restful after long afternoon of too bright and too hot.

It makes it look cool, that the sky has started to darken and yard is in deep shadow.

June emails

Anne emails her friends from womens lib

Sunday afternoon June 9th

Hi girls

It is Sunday afternoon, the heat is great but the breezes make it bearable.

The beauty makes it a joy to look out my open window

I swam at noon and then came home and watched the *Perry Mason* marathon for the rest of the afternoon. It is now 5 pm. LOL the morning doves announced it and the first of them is arriving in my yard.

It's not that my life has stopped exactly since the big heat arrived several days ago.

But my life sure has down-sized or minimized. My driving lessons have stopped. I am down to swimming and that's all.

I have stopped my projects on the computer too, the most I do is go on FaceBook. When there is nothing to watch on TV I spend a lot of time on FaceBook. But with the *Perry Mason* marathon this weekend, I haven't been on it at all.

Maybe it is just a time-out. I didn't know that life provides time-outs, but I see now it does.

I was fine all day yesterday till late in the evening when suddenly I got bummed out by the emptiness of my life.

LOL I actually cried.

But I woke up this morning fine.

Jim imitated my driving yesterday morning when he took me to Mac's Indian Jewelry store to buy myself a new Navajo ring because I lost one of mine.

Even tho I was laughing at his imitation— it was so familiar to me everything he was doing, I recognized my own driving.

It was such a horrible bumpy, jostling, effort filled, nerve wracking ride.

I had no idea I put Jim thru that each time I drive.

When he drives it is always smooth as silk.

I laughed the whole time he did it, which I guess encouraged him to keep it up.

But secretly I was dismayed and discouraged. I have never driven with a terrible driver before, it makes for such an awful ride.

I had no idea I was that bad!

Love and kisses, Annie

Jim nearly goes thru the windshield each time I drive

Email Tuesday June 11 night

Well this evening has been an enjoyable respite from television.

LOL maybe my mind has finished its time-out.

The dull stupor I was in from the heat has lifted.

This evening I watched some TV. Then came in and found wonderful emails from all of you and emailed with you the rest of the evening.

It's almost time for the George Burns and Gracie Allen show now. That Gracie is sure fun!!!

I told Jim in the car yesterday that George said "Gracie takes such good care of our car. Every night Gracie goes to the garage to let the air out of the tires, so in the morning they can have fresh air."

Jim turned to me in all seriousness and said "If *you* do that I'll murder you."

I was so surprised. I never realized Jim thinks I am a nitwit.

Well almost time for Gracie.

June 12 early morning

How I bought Irene's painting

I realize now I never told anyone the story of how I bought Irene's painting, not even my husband. Because it happened during one of my ordeals before I left NYC. And no one wants to remember their ordeals.

I bought the painting from Irene the summer before I moved to Tucson, which would be summer of 1991. I did not know I was going to move to Tucson at the time.

We moved to Tucson on Thanksgiving 1991. And when we bought this house a year later, I paid Irene to ship it to us. It had not left Irene's apt. till then.

Her husband Richard took it to the store which ships things.

And Bill put it up on the wall. It was before he went to art school and became an artist himself.

He said "It makes our house so classy that we have a painting by a New York modern artist."

When he was going to art school he was sleeping on the couch underneath that painting.

He said he would look up at it and learn from it.

And it was while he was sleeping under that painting— he had finished art school now, and was trying to be an artist on his own, and torturing himself about how to start painting on his own— that he heard his Higher Self speak to him for the first time.

I guess he was torturing himself that he had to paint something good, which was paralyzing him.

So the first thing his Higher Self said to him was "You are learning."

Which meant he doesn't have to paint something good, just to learn from doing it.

It really helped Bill because he took the pressure off himself as a result.

I myself had discovered my Higher Self (heard Her for the first time) the day before I went to Irene's apartment way over in the West Village and saw that painting over her dining room table.

I had gone over there because Irene called me up in

tears. My Higher Self said "Tell her you'll be right over." Then my Higher Self told me to take a taxi cab and come right over to her house.

While we were having lunch and I was looking up at the painting, my Higher Self said "Tell her you want to buy it, you will give her one thousand dollars for it." Irene was overjoyed. It is the first painting I ever bought.

LOL I guess my Higher Self doesn't fool around. When your friend calls you up desperate and in tears, your Higher Self has you hop into a cab right away and buy her new painting for $1000. Irene was a totally happy girl when I left.

I was in the midst of an incredible ordeal myself at the time, which is why and how I had just discovered my Higher Self.

It thrilled me to my toes to buy a painting for $1000, never would I have imagined I would do that!

That was before I even bought myself any new clothes. I was still buying all my clothes for $1 from the homeless on the street.

I guess this is what they mean when they say "Your Higher Self knows the past, present, and future of everyone involved."

Who knew I was going to move to Tucson few months later! Who knew Bill was going to go to art school in Tucson! Or that we would have a house!

I liked buying the painting at the time because it was such a shock to me that I had done that. And it sure cheered up Irene, she was totally happy girl when I left.

But looking back on it all, I think it is the best $1000 I ever spent. After all, in Tucson we got our first car (the truck I am learning to drive on now) and discovered the wonderful world of car repair. It is always $1000.

Irene's painting is still up on my living room after all these years.

I met Irene in the womens liberation movement too. That is where we all met each other and Irene.

We were wild chicks back in the days of womens liberation

Now we try to help each other on email

Rolling Over Curbs

Sent: Thursday, June 13, 2013 7:24 AM
To: Jean and Peggy and Ruthie and Pat and Casey and Heather and Jo
Subject: a few mistakes while driving this morning...

This morning I drove around my neighborhood again for first time since serious heat arrived.

I decided to stop at one of the stop signs just the way the examiner will want me to do it on the road test.

A little behind the sign, instead of in front of it.

"How's that?" I asked Jim, "perfect, right?" I said.

"Except you're on the curb" he said.

"I am??" I said.

"Yes" he said.

"No problem" I said.

Since I was on tiny hill I simply let my foot off the brake and clutch and let it roll back slowly off the curb.

"Well whaddya know it worked" I said, "perfect, right?" I said.

"Except when you're letting the car roll backwards, you're supposed to look to see that there is no other car right behind you."

"Ooops!" I said.

Ooops

The girls email back to me and to each other

from Casey

hee hee. so much to remember!

i wouldn't want to be learning to drive in a truck, tho.... I could hardly drive ours and I've been driving for over 50 years...

from Peggy

I still drive up on curbs and fail to turn around to check. Of course, I still have an accident from time to time

from Jean

Oh hell I roll over curbs all the time, clutch or no clutch. They're just there to slow you down!

from Casey

I roll over curbs, too...

hard on the vehicle, tho...

from Ruthie

I did it so much that I had to buy entirely new rims for the car

Later that month

From: Annie
To: Jean and Peggy and Ruthie and Pat and Casey and Heather and Jo
Subject: I am pulled over for being a suspect

Anne is surprised

I got pulled over by a cop. But I hadn't done anything

wrong this time. So he was nice to me and did not give me

a ticket.

He pulled me over because a lady reported "a truck is going very slowly and she is looking at houses." So he tracked me down.

Officer Herford looked the same age as my big cousin John. He was completely relaxed and easy going with me. And did not care one bit that I got out of my truck barefoot to go over and ask him a question.

And stood there chitchatting with him.

LOL I guess they sent in their most experienced cop to track down the suspect.

Jim and I still had to sit there a long time while he called in to make sure we were who we said we were and truck was not stolen etc.

So there was not much time left when I arrived for my swim. Still it was so nice to swim.

And then I treated Jim and me to take-out fast food Mexican. I wanted to give Jim a treat. It upsets him so much when I get pulled over by the cops because they take his license too and examine it and call in about it, etc.

Plus neither of us wears seatbelt and he worries they will fine each of us $200.

While driving to the pool I said to Jim, "He was a lot

nicer than Officer Jeffries. She does not belong on the force."

"She belongs on my lap!" he said.

Jim is turned on by Officer Jeffries long legs

It is time for Anne to learn to drive in traffic
And it's not working out

She flounces out of the car when she gets upset

And then they have a fight

3 way conversation me and Jim and God

Such an interesting driving lesson this morning.

Yesterday I was willing to drive out of the neighborhood to 2 destinations. God had suggested it. But on the way there were 2 fights with Jim. Because he told me to do one thing, and God said do another.

And Jim was mad that I didn't listen to him. "You have to listen to me!" he said.

The problem is that Jim goes by my driving skills. When he said "Do it! You can do it!" he believes it.

But God lives inside me and knows when I am too scared to do it.

So He says "don't do it."

I always listen to God.

Even tho Jim says "You can do it! You have to do it! You

have to trust me!"

I don't trust him. I trust God.

Because I know the instant something scares me while I am driving, my mind shuts down, I forget to keep my foot on the clutch, the car stalls. Then I get even more nervous, and I have trouble starting it up again.

Jim has no idea why I suddenly have problems. He doesn't know what scares me.

He doesn't know what makes me nervous. Sometimes it is something he says.

I never tell him that it is something he said that made me nervous and that caused me to have problems.

Because I know in my heart of hearts that even tho Jim is the best driver in the world, he has no experience in teaching. I am the first one he has tried to teach anything to.

He is learning to teach, I am learning to drive.

But I know how to teach, I know the only way Jim can be a better teacher is by having confidence in his teaching.

So I never tell him when something he is telling me has a boomerang effect on me. Makes things worse instead of better. Makes it harder for me to learn to drive.

But driving in traffic is serious. And it is now time for me to start to do it.

When I woke up this morning, I knew we had to have a 3 way conversation about it, him and me and God. God had to give him helpful suggestions.

We sat down to have the conversation when Jim arrived, right before driving me to DMV so I could practice tushy turns there.

Altho Jim said he agreed to the conversation, right after God told him how much He loved him and appreciated what he was doing in teaching me how to drive, the instant God tried to talk to Jim seriously about how to help me with driving in traffic.

Jim simply refused to listen. He kept saying "This is waste of time, let's go!"

This is the third time there has been a 3 way between me and Jim and God.

The first two times were early on in my driving lessons. And the conversation took place on the phone in the afternoon, when God said "call him and tell him I want to talk to him."

Both times Jim kept trying to get off the phone instantly and both times he began fighting with God. And both times God responded by changing his tune from the originally sweet loving tender tone he has begun with by getting tough with Jim in response.

So Jim gets tougher and God gets tougher, and I always think "this is going to end in disaster."

I always think "how can this work if Jim and God are fighting with each other."

I'm always so stunned that Jim is fighting with God. Whoever heard of anyone fighting with God, thinking they can possibly bully their way thru it.

So this morning by now both sides were shouting. And God was saying "Stop being obstreperous."

That caught Jim by surprise. "What does obstreperous mean?" he asked.

Every time God tried to talk Jim interrupted and would not let God speak.

When God did try to talk, Jim either said "you're wrong" or "I already do that."

Finally God said "You have to sit still and shut up. I want to finish what I have to say. When I finish you can comment."

I think Jim was very surprised that God told him to shut up.

It's interesting to notice now that at no point did Jim think it was me saying all this, he did believe it was God saying all this thru me. Because if he had believed it was me saying this, he would have been very mad at me. He would have enraged himself at me.

Instead he kept saying to me "Let's go!"

God finally did manage to say his piece very quickly. And then we got in the truck and took off for DMV.

Interestingly when we were driving, maybe driving relaxed Jim or being on our way relaxed him, he got receptive to the conversation.

Because to my surprise God said a lot of things to Jim that he was totally receptive to hearing.

I don't know if he was receptive to anything God said while we were sitting on the two chairs in front of my house. I mean I don't know if Jim was willing to hear any of it.

But while we were driving and there was no heat in the conversation, Jim was receptive, and God was able to express himself in such a calm way.

And Jim was able to recognize how sensible it all was, and helpful.

He stopped being defensive. He was willing to take it in.

As a result God was able to express himself to Jim in a much kinder more loving way too.

It was a conversation which worked.

And the odd thing is how much it liberated both of us. I felt Jim now understood where I was at, God had explained it to him perfectly.

And Jim understood where I was at and God had helpfully explained the best way to handle it in simple practical terms.

Jim could now know what to do and what not to do when I am driving in traffic. And he was able to understand what happened and why it happened, and responded to God's suggestions of how to get around it.

"Don't press Anne to make the light," God said. "It's better for her to be stopped at red light. She is so tense driving, it gives her a moment to relax, calm down and get herself organized.

"Being stopped at a red light is good for Anne right now.

"If she starts to drive slowly because she doesn't know where the driveway is for her to pull into at the Y or somewhere else, don't press her to go faster because she is holding up the cars behind her.

"It just makes her nervous when you tell her she is holding everyone up, she gets flustered and stalls."

Jim said "I'll just let the cars behind her honk at her."

And God said "Brilliant! Good idea! She'll find out she is holding up traffic that way. It will be a genuine learning experience in driving.

"Don't make her make that right turn on Columbus on red light, the lanes are too close together. You always have to grab the wheel because she comes too close to hitting car in the other lane waiting for the light.

"Let her wait till the light is green, then she doesn't have to dart if cars are coming, and can just focus on making that turn."

God also said, "When she drives around the neighborhood she is so relaxed it is perfect time to fine tune all her driving. She appreciates all the correction and learns from it.

"But when she is driving in traffic don't say anything. Unless it is actually dangerous. Remember everything she did wrong and then when you switch seats you can tell her.

"Or better yet. Just say good job. Let her relax. Buy her an ice cold coca cola. Let her have a cigarette, and then after that tell her everything she did wrong.

"But maybe start off with saying she did a good job. In fact tell her she made progress. Anne does not believe that she makes progress at all, she never thinks she is getting anywhere. Tell her she is making progress, and then gently point out to her the things she did wrong. She does need to know that.

"Just give her a chance to relax and unwind first so she can take it in."

God did say "You tell Anne what she can do based on her skills, but I live inside her and I know what scares her.

"I want Anne to go out of her comfort zone now but it is not helpful for her to be scared. It's not necessary. And because I know what scares her it is better if she listens to me."

Miraculously this conversation in the car really did work like a charm. It made it possible for Jim and I to understand each other and cooperate when it came to driving.

He had more confidence in me, I had more confidence in him, we were more relaxed and easygoing with each other. I noticed the change when he stopped for gas on our way to DMV and I sat on the curb to smoke a cigarette.

It was more than giving each other the benefit of the doubt. We were on the same page. I trusted him. He trusted me. We both knew beyond a shadow of a doubt how well intentioned we were towards each other. We became more assertive with each other in a natural way. Instead of irritating each other we harmonized.

When we got to DMV I did 6 tushy turns in a row.

And then God suggested I drive the route that the examiner will have me drive. Jim was all for it. He guided me on the route.

I made my turn onto 22nd Street (a major boulevard) and drove very slowly in the slow lane. I just switched to second gear, I didn't try to switch to third.

Jim said "Turn at the light."

The light was red and there were no cars coming in any direction.

"I'm going to turn on red" I said. And I did.

And I turned into the neighborhood.

Jim started to say something and said "I will wait till you are done."

But I was so relaxed driving in the neighborhood I said "tell me now, I am relaxed."

He said "You have to stop at the red light, and not just keep on going to make your turn. What you did is called running a red light."

I was so pleased to hear it. I was glad to learn that. I really hadn't known it.

And I thought it was so sweet of Jim to listen to God and try not to tell me while I am driving.

My trust and confidence in him shot up a whole notch. And I bet it was mutual.

After we finished driving in the neighborhood, God suggested, "Do 22nd Street again. Do the whole thing again."

God said "Ask Jim what he suggests, should you do 22nd Street again or just drive back to DMV and park like you will have to do on the test."

Jim thought and said "Do 22nd Street, it is the harder thing."

"That's just what God suggested, you both agree.

"I am willing to do it, I'm going to be big brave girl. Should I ask you or God to give me pat on the back?"

And Jim gave me pat on the back.

Jim said "eventually you're going to have to switch to third on 22nd Street, the examiner will want to see that you know how to do that."

I said "God said I shouldn't try that now, I have enuf on my plate while I drive 22nd Street, but absolutely you're right I have to learn to do that. Either next time or the time after that."

So I drove 22nd Street again, the neighborhood again. And Jim reminded me that I had told him God said I should switch to third gear on the long empty stretch to 22nd Street.

"Good!" I said.

"You have to practice that" he said.

"Good" I said. "You are right."

And when I reached 22nd Street, I said "God said do it again," and Jim said "great!" And I did it all again.

And I switched to third for the long stretch on the road which leads to 22nd Street and we switched seats.

I said "God said we should both be rewarded. And you stop at 7/11 and let me treat you and me to a Coca Cola. Will you let me buy you one?"

"Yes" he said.

"What about a donut too?"

"Yes" he said.

And you know I think we were the happiest boy and girl in the world as he drove and I sat in passenger seat, and we were both perfectly satisfied with ourselves and each other.

It is really quite amazing, the last two times I had tried to drive in traffic, we had huge fight in the car.

This time it was all sweet as sugar.

Our happiness driving together went up a whole other notch.

I wonder if what changed it was when God said while we first started driving to DMV, "You know Jim, Anne's driving is not the most important thing, the most important thing is you two getting along.

"Because Anne really loves you, not as a boyfriend, as a friend and it distresses her too much when you fight. She doesn't want to be upset with you.

"And Anne's happiness is the most important thing in the world, not her driving, so no matter what I don't want you two to fight."

I think after that is when Jim became totally receptive to everything God had to say about the driving.

I don't know why, but I think it was what turned the corner.

Anne is relaxed at the pool after her driving lesson

I Drive to Indian Jewelry Store

Today began my second week of actually driving. I have now driven to the pool at the Y and back home from the pool at the Y every day for whole week.

So this morning when I woke up and noticed the stone had fallen out of my Navajo bracelet. I love Navajo jewelry and now have bracelets on each wrist, and rings on each finger. But just one necklace.

I wear the jewelry all the time (when I sleep, when I swim) so some of it I got reinforced at Mac's Indian Jewelry where I bought it all.

As I said to Jim when I got out of the truck with the bracelet with its missing stone, "Let's hope I just give it to her to be fixed and don't buy anything new.

"Navajo jewelry is my passion. But I should not be

spending money right now."

Almost immediately after Bill went to Heaven, I had Jim drive me to Mac's Indian Jewelry, that is when I bought beautiful rings for every finger and beautiful new bracelets.

I did not care about money one bit when Bill went to Heaven, being happy was all that mattered to me.

I kept that up for two years. It was a very long shopping spree. Since Jim had to drive me everywhere back then I would say "it is my birthday present." He did start to complain about driving me for 97 birthday presents.

The shopping spree ended last month when I got hit with a very expensive car repair. But I still buy myself some treats some times.

Which works out perfectly. Now that driving is the big adventure in my life, I don't need shopping for adventure. And cooling it with shopping has simplified my life.

So I decided when I woke up this morning that when Jim arrived for me to drive, instead of just driving to my Y pool, I would drive to Mac's Indian Jewelry first.

The idea of driving there scared me of course but I remembered that God had said "You have to be willing to go out of your comfort zone now.

"And a destination is a good way to do it."

We got in the truck and I told Jim the route I planned to take. He said "OK."

It's just that the store is on Grant Road and I am not willing to drive on Grant Road yet. But I was willing to drive on Tucson Blvd which I have never driven on before.

The store is on Grant Road just a half block down on Tucson Blvd.

I had no idea how I was going to maneuver it.

I was on Tucson Blvd approaching Grant Road when I decided I would turn off to the left onto some little road right behind the store. I thought "I'll figure out what I will do then.

"Maybe I can just park it there and walk."

Tucson (I see now that I am driving) has a turn lane in between lanes.

So I signaled left that I was going into the turn lane and then started to look for a tiny road very close to Grant Road to turn left into that.

There was no incoming traffic at all in the lane I had to go thru to get to a little road.

Maybe I thought I had seen a little road because I was now in the lane of the incoming traffic driving slowly along looking for a tiny road to turn into. There was still no incoming traffic as I was driving along in the wrong lane looking.

Jim got hysterical. "You're driving in the wrong lane!" he kept yelling at me.

I knew I was driving in the wrong lane.

"Turn off now!" he kept saying, "you're driving in the wrong lane! Officer Jeffries would give you a million tickets for this!"

I was still crawling along in the wrong lane looking for a turn off which was as close to the store as I could get because I knew I would have to walk to the store. But he could not stand me crawling along in wrong lane.

I was ignoring his yelling at me. Finally he reached over for the wheel himself and I pulled into a gas station on the corner.

It was the perfect solution. I had no idea there was a gas station on the corner. I just drove thru it to the parking lot to the next building with the deserted building, no one in the parking lot.

It turned out to be right next door to Mac's Indian Jewelry but there was a blockade so I couldn't drive thru it to the parking lot for Mac's Indian Jewelry, so I parked and went in.

He was still having an hysteria that I drove in the wrong lane.

I said "You know the girls in my womens lib group that I am on email with are all super duper drivers, and they would never carry on if I did this with them. They would find it normal.

"They are not a baby like you who has a fit about everything."

I really must be whole lot more relaxed about driving if I could tease Jim about his fit this way. In the past I went into total anxiety tension when I did something wrong while driving.

This time I brushed it off and teased him about it.

"Don't let me buy anything new in there, I love Navajo jewelry, I just want my bracelet fixed," I said as I was getting out of the car.

He waited for me in the passenger seat in the deserted parking lot.

I walked in and the only one in whole store was Karen, the owner of the store. I love her and she loves me.

First I showed her the bracelet and gave it to her for her repairman to fix.

Then I looked at the pretty bracelets which were on a

thing sticking up on the counter.

"Do you think this one is pretty?" I asked her

"Yes" she said.

"What about this one?" I asked.

"Yes that is pretty too."

One said 95 on price tag, one said 75.

"Which one do you think is prettier?"

She looked for long time.

And chose the one which cost less money.

"I know I shouldn't be buying anything" I said to her, "I just had an expensive car repair.

"But O this silver bangle is so sparkly and pretty.

"Do you think I should get it too?"

I said to her "I know you want to sell bracelets, but also you love me, so you will tell me what is best for me."

She looked at both my hands, the bracelets I had on each wrist and studied the ones I already had on there.

She said "The one with the beads would look good here. And silver bangle would look good here, it is up to you."

The silver bangle was 96 but she said she would take off 20.

And the one with little stones threaded around was 75, she said she would take off 20. She said "I would have to charge sales tax tho." And she got out her little calculator.

"It would cost you $120 for both of them" she said.

"O what the heck" I said "you only live once and I love both of them, I'll get them both.

"Will you reinforce the one with the little stones threaded around so I can wear it for swimming and sleeping."

"Yes" she said.

"I'll pay for it all then, when I come back for my bracelet repaired."

"You will have to pay for the new stone" she said.

"That is OK" I said.

I was really happy with my purchases.

I really had not planned to buy new bracelets and I am overjoyed.

I got back in the drivers seat of the truck. "Of course I bought 2 new bracelets" I said to Jim

"O no!" he said "you can't afford it."

I said "Let's switch seats. You just take it across Grant Road for me back onto Tucson Boulevard and I will drive down Tucson Blvd to Glenn and take it to the club."

"Watch how I do this!" he said. "Pay close attention, it is easy and you can learn."

(But God told me "you don't have to pay close attention, it is too advanced for you." So I only glanced at corner of my eye.)

But the instant Jim got it across Grant Road and onto Tucson Blvd, I said "pull in somewhere so I can drive it to my club."

"You can pull in here" I said

"O you missed it! OK pull in here then!"

"Are you saying you are a better driver than I am?"

"Of course" I said. "I am better than you at everything."

Then we switched seats in that parking lot, and I drove it to Glenn, turned left on Glenn to go to Columbus. My Y is on Columbus.

For the first time while I was driving in traffic I was willing to have conversation with him while I drive. Usually I am too tense and concentrating too hard.

"No conversation in the car while I am driving!" I say when he brings up a topic.

But this time I teased him the whole way about how he carried on about me driving in the wrong lane.

"The girls in my womens lib group that I am on email with would never have acted up about it," I said.

"Well let them be the ones to drive with you," he said.

"I can't wait till you have your license and I don't have to do this anymore."

"What happened" I said, "when you first began teaching me how to drive, you were so gung-ho about it, you were so enthusiastic, you loved it so much. You said when any of my friends from NYC move to Tucson you want to teach them to drive too.

"You wanted to teach Linda Feldman how to drive and she has never even been in a car in her whole life.

"Are you saying that after teaching me how to drive for 2 and a half years you are no longer so enthusiastic about it."

He said "I am never going to teach anyone to drive again."

LOL I think my driving instructor has had it.

Also I noticed the whole time I was driving there and driving home, he sticks out his hands and holds on to the dash before I even begin driving to brace himself.

He knows what a bumpy ride he will have.

But guess what! On the drive home from the pool I lapsed into conversation while I was driving. I know that route so well now, and have driven it every day for past week.

It is the very first time Jim and I chatted on the way home.

I teased him about winning all the bets on football games this season.

I said "I will win every pro game, every college game, every high school game in Arizona, and then win Super Bowl.

"I will give you deposit slip for my credit union, you can put all the money you lose to me right in my bank."

Instead of driving home in total tense concentration and forcing Jim not to open his mouth, I actually chatted all the way up Columbus.

And did not get silent till 5th Street.

"When do I move into the turn lane? Is this OK?" I asked.

"Fine" he said "do it now."

And I turned into the little alley which borders my house and parked in my own driveway.

Success! For everything I put Jim thru I think he is secretly proud. After all it was 2 and a half years with zero progress at all. He is just as stunned and happy as I am that finally I am actually driving.

Monday September 9th

Wonderful Day

I would say my wonderful day began when we first arrived on the little road which leads to DMV. Because that is where Jim pulled over so we could change seats.

And when I got out of the passenger seat to walk around truck to driver seat, I emerged exactly where wildflowers were growing up by the side of the road.

I have no idea why the wildflowers flourish there and it is so green. My yards are dry as a bone, there are no wildflowers and no tall green grasses around them.

And when I looked down there was one wildflower I have never seen before in my life. It was so tall and thin, it's a miracle my eyes were able to focus on it.

Just a sliver of white loveliness. But it took my breath away. "I feel so blessed," I said to Jim and I meant it.

The tushy turns at the DMV were stressful for me and I did not enjoy them one bit. But it was no big deal and I just looked forward to them being over, so I could drive the route the examiner will take me on my road test.

It is the brand new thing in my life that now I actually enjoy driving. I was looking forward to finishing up my practice tushy turns so I would be free to leave and drive on the road again.

And I did become very happy as soon as I was driving. It is the first time I have driven that route at DMV since driving in traffic took off for me last week.

I was no longer scared little rabbit driving along 22nd Street. I am now used to driving with others on the road. And am even getting used to negotiating the road.

And I was so happy sailing along in that neighborhood the examiner will have me drive thru, that I drove with one hand perfectly relaxed and chatted my head off with Jim and kidded around.

I've driven that neighborhood so often now it is piece of cake for me. And of course now I am a driver who has driven in real traffic on the road. Residential driving is a total cinch for me.

I drove the whole route 3 times. And Jim and I kidded

around a lot.

The last house you pass before you get back to area around DMV and begin the route again had an older couple, a man and woman, standing curbside in front of their house. She was spraying the weeds.

I called out to them "I am learning how to drive!" And they waved and smiled.

So naturally Jim teased me each time I was going to arrive past their house again that they are inside their house barricaded to be safe from me.

And of course I teased Jim "I wonder if the examiner will be upset with me if I run over the little old man and the little old lady."

Altho I kept making mistakes when Jim suggested I drive back to the DMV when it was over because the examiner will have me do that.

I loused it up so badly that I said to Jim "next time we come here I will practice that."

O that's right! Then there was the drama of me trying to make my U turn to get out of DMV parking lot instead of driving all the way thru it and around.

I guess there wasn't enuf room for me to make my U turn altho I tried a few times. And every time I went in reverse to give myself more room, I botched it.

After a lot of botches I finally got it and drove Jim almost to the intersection of 22nd Street, so we could change seats for Jim to drive us to pool.

Adventures at Discount Bedding

Anne enjoys herself at Discount Bedding

While we were stuck in that place at DMV when I couldn't figure out how to get out of it, I said "We may as well stop here for a moment and figure out what we are going to do now.

"Look at your clock" I said.

So Jim got out his cell phone and said "it is two minutes before noon."

I said "Two minutes before noon! And my bedding store, Tuesday Morning, opens at noon! And when I gave you its address you said it is very close to here. Let's go!"

And I got very excited. I said to Jim, "I know I should not be buying myself presents now, I know I should not be spending money. On the other hand I love presents, so I guess the thing is to strike a balance."

And I got so excited that we were going to go to Tuesday Morning, which is discount bedding store and happens to be one of my favorite stores.

I haven't been there since Bill went to Heaven because I never wanted to make Jim drive me there. And I discovered I can order from them on the internet. And so for the past two years I have been ordering from them on the internet.

When you order on internet I have now discovered you have no idea what it will look like in real life. A tiny photo on internet is almost more of a hint of what it could look like. It is always a total surprise what actually does arrive.

But I was always happy with my surprises from Tuesday Morning, they were different from what I imagined but always better than I imagined.

So I was not happy when I read two weeks ago they are no longer selling on internet, now you have to go to the store.

So I looked up the addresses for their stores in Tucson, they are no longer where they used to be. And I wrote both down for Jim to take me to one of them. And Jim said "one is close to the DMV" and so I had it in mind to go there.

But because this has been the strangest month in my whole life (one car repair after another, it never stopped) we haven't been back to DMV on a Sunday to practice tushy turns in long time.

Yesterday was the first time.

It's amazing how excited I got about going to a store. Other than buying food I haven't been to a store for long time.

I was in Mac's Indian Jewelry two weeks ago, but that is not a store where you can walk around and grab anything which catches your fancy. And I hadn't planned to buy anything when I went there, just to get my bracelet repaired.

Tuesday Morning is a lot like walking into a grab-bag. You have no idea what will be there and it's all stuff to catch your fancy. It is a little girl's dream come true, or big girl's too.

And in their outside bins before I even entered the store were thick drinking glasses. I have been using empty jam jars for my juice in the morning or my soda at night. I thought "this is better than a pickle jar." And chose two. And next to it was a bin of straw purses.

I had had an urge for new pocketbook and looked at Lane Bryant's sale on them on internet over weekend. And they had a pretty straw one which looked big enuf for everything I would want to put in it. But which was $40. That was a lot more than I wanted to spend.

But here was a straw one for $5 and because it was right before my eyes I could know what size it actually was.

Last year at this time I ordered a very cute purse from Lane Bryant and when it arrived my wallet would not fit in it. So it sits on my door knob.

I didn't want to make that booboo again.

There was a little shopping cart right there so I put the straw bag and two thick drinking glasses in it and wheeled it over to bedding.

But on the way sunglasses caught my eye, and two were so cute, I put them in the cart to make up my mind at the check out.

Bedding did have beautiful sheet sets at very discounted prices, I put two in my cart to make up my mind at check out.

And then I saw their pocketbook selection. Pocketbooks are my weakness. I really want a new pocketbook.

The cutest one was a very small persimmon one. I love that color. I put it in my shopping cart to decide at check out.

While on line at check-out I got my wallet out of my own pocketbook and put it in their persimmon one and to my surprise and delight it fitted. I decided to buy it.

"I can't decide between the two sheet sets" I said to her. "One is $69 and one is $79."

"They are both 69," she said. "O good!" I said. "Which one do you think is best?"

In the past I had always gone to the Tuesday Morning which used to be near my house. The girl who worked there, Norma, always knew what I liked and what would make me happy and was such an expert about everything in the stock.

All I needed to say to her is "which one should I get?" and in an instant she would point to the right one and that was always the one which made me perfectly happy.

I guess this woman at check-out was used to customers who know what they want. She was so sweet and sincere and tried so hard to help.

She read off the description from each package. And even opened both up so I could feel each one to see which one I liked the feel of better.

"They are both a good brand" she said.

I said "this one feels silkier, who does not want silk sheets!"

But the woman who was waiting her turn at the next cashier, helped me out instantly. "That is the good one, get that one."

"Thank you" I said. "Thank you."

She had been behind me on line when the other cashier arrived. And I said "Good! I am someone you don't want to be behind on line!"

But she hadn't seemed to mind being behind me. When I had tried fitting my wallet in the persimmon purse, I said to the lady ahead of me being waited on, "I have to see if it fits.

"Else it sits on my door knob forever."

Which is true. I just turned my head and there it is. Cute as a button and on my doorknob. It has never left my door knob.

That lady had not responded, pursed her lips and looked away. But this girl, who looked just like the girls back in NYC who were my type, was responding enthusiastically and with friendly interest to everything I was saying to anyone.

I asked my cashier what she thought of the purse.

"I like the color" she said.

"Me too. That is why I chose it. What do you call this color?" I asked her. "Flamingo? Persimmon?"

"Salmon" she said. "It's a favorite color of mine" she said.

"Me too, it's one of my favorite colors."

And then she helped me with the sunglasses. I tried on each one for her and said "which is better for me?"

One made everything blurry when I put it on and I couldn't see. She said "that one will interfere with your vision."

I said "I'm learning how to drive so I have to have sunglasses which work well."

She was so sweet and darling and gave everything such careful attention. She said "those ones will be good, they cover more."

"I'll get them" I said.

Altho to myself I thought "I need sunglasses like a hole in the head." I just bought a pair at Walgreens last week and I never wear any of my pairs of sunglasses. I am afraid I won't see as well while I am driving if I wear them.

When it was all finished I saw I had all my copies of *Pulled Over By The Cops* in my purse. I said "Do you like to read? This is a present. I wrote it." She shook her head no, said she does not like to read.

So I turned instantly to that wonderful girl, who had been so interested and so involved in everything I was doing. With her shopping cart filled with every chatchka in the store.

"Do you like to read?" I asked her.

I was still holding the book in my hand.

"I love to read" she said.

"Would you like it?"

"I would love it!" she said. I went out of my mind with joy.

I handed it to her. And she looked at the cover. And saw

the title *Pulled Over By The Cops* and the cartoon Bill did of girl crying on the curb I had put on the cover.

And she said "I can tell already this is going to be fun."

And she handed it back to me saying "will you please autograph it for me."

I was thrilled.

I borrowed one of the lady cashier's pens. I said "what is your name?"

She said "Nina" and she spelled it.

"N-I-N-A" she said.

"O I know" I said, "my best friend from childhood was named Nina."

So I wrote "To Nina. I love you. Annie."

And handed her back the book. She was so excited, "You have made my day" she said.

"You made my day," I said.

I was thrilled she wanted my book.

LOL in the past 4 years I have now published 5 or 6 books and it has started to dawn on me that only two people have bought a copy of any of my books in all this time.

I find myself doing something like an algebra equation in my head. X plus Y is 4. What is X?

I think "Is it that people don't like to read?"

But I see people reading books around me all the time.

So then I think "Is it my books, do they not deliver the joy people want to find in books?"

LOL giggle giggle I am always looking for the X factor.

For a long time I didn't pay attention to the fact that no one bought my books.

But maybe because I have spent the past 3 months trying to edit this one and been having such a hard time with it. The train of thought which begins when I mute my TV show during a commercial begins with an idea of how I might edit this book.

And always ends with "What is the X factor? How come no one wants to read my books?"

Anyway this is all to explain why I went into total ecstasy when Nina yesterday was so overjoyed to get my book to read.

Nothing in the whole world could have made me happier.

And it came at the perfect time.

But it wasn't only about her being happy to get my book.

I couldn't believe my luck that I had bumped into a girl

just like me in Tucson.

She looked and acted just like all my friends back in NYC. She and I clicked. We really did.

She was as happy to meet me as I was happy to meet her.

We wound up wheeling our carts out of Tuesday Morning at the same time and I brought her right over to introduce her to Jim.

And then we each said to each other again, "you made my whole day." Which was sure true for me.

Because when I got back in the truck with Jim with all my purchases (I was so excited about my purchases) I was totally thrilled about having met Nina.

I was so surprised he was not into Nina. Jim is totally into women. Ordinarily he would have been so excited to be introduced to a beautiful woman.

And I would have heard all about her legs. She was wearing shorts.

In fact I would have heard all about her all the way home.

But a very peculiar thing has happened since I began actually driving last week, after two and a half years with zero progress at all.

Jim is so excited about me actually driving, that he is totally involved in giving me driving tips now.

He couldn't have been less interested in Nina. "What a wonderful girl!" I said as soon as I got in my passenger seat. "I am so happy I met her."

"This is Jim" I had said to her when I introduced her, "he is my friend who is teaching me how to drive. He is the other character in my book and when you read it you will know all his secrets."

Can you believe that did not interest Jim at all!

Instead the first thing he said to me is "Look!

"Do you see how the truck and all the cars in the parking lot are reflected in the store window. You treat that as a mirror and use it when you pull out."

I was still lost in the glory of meeting Nina. I was not interested at all in using the store window as a mirror on how to pull out of the parking lot.

When he saw my lack of attention, he thought I didn't follow what he said. And tried to say it again.

So I returned my attention to him. "I get it" I said. "Use it as a mirror."

"Exactly" he said.

"It's a good tip for you" he said.

"Thank you Jim" I said.

And then we each went into our own worlds and talked happily about what interests us both.

Jim talked about driving tips all the way to the pool and I said how much I like Nina and wonderful time I had in the store.

Mi Casa

To: Jean, Peggy, Heather, Jo, Pat, Ruthie, Casey
Sent: Tuesday, September 17, 2013 7:49 PM
Subject: LOL evicting the black widows

It was a beautiful sunset this evening, the clouds turned pink at sunset.

Frank arrived to evict the black widows from my bedroom. I hadn't realized they were so close to my bed. And that the huge one under the TV was still there.

I actually screamed when Frank saw a big one next to the cover I had pushed to the floor last night because it was too warm.

Frank's helper, Miguel, was with him (they were doing yard work for me). And both boys found it so much fun when I screamed.

LOL I haven't acted like a "girl" in long time, and completely forgot how exciting boys found it. Which is probably how I got into it in the first place as a young teenager.

Love Annie

Cupcake goes too far

To: Jan
Sent: Wednesday, September 11, 2013 7:26 PM
Subject: O Jan this time Cupcake went too far

O Jan if only there were a 12 Step program Murderers Anonymous for Cats.

I put up with the lizards, I put up with the baby birds.

But I just got up to turn the lights on in the house, it is starting to get dark

And there is a baby bunny rabbit on the carpet. Cupcake is a murderer of bunnies now!!!

I had no idea bunnies are coming into my backyard. And I would have had such joy watching them hopping about.

Now I feel like I should post a sign,

Bunnies Beware
Killer cat lives here

I just saw Cupcake and I gave her such a dirty look!

I don't want to be mad at Cupcake, I love Cupcake. But

I'm not going to serve her her favorite treats this evening.

Tomorrow will be a new day, she can have her favorite treats tomorrow.

I wish you and Harry a lovely evening.

I love you

Annie

From: Jan
To: Annie
Sent: Thursday, September 12, 2013 8:56 PM
Subject: Re: O Jan this time Cupcake went too far!!

Anne, cats will be cats. It is their instinct and they don't understand our aversion to it. Cupcake should meet Oreo, one of our neighbor's cats who was the terror of the neighborhood until she got older and sticks around the house. Birds, lizards, bunnies, anything that moved.

Yet she is a great cat, loving with loads of personality and has given Joan, our neighbor, and us great love and joy.

Love,

Jan

October 1   Tuesday   11 am

I passed my drivers test

The plan was for Jim to come at 8 am for us to go to DMV. But I was up for few hours in middle of night.

Altho I had been anxious about it all day yesterday, finally my Higher Self said, "You will do your best. You can't do better than your best. And however it turns out will be for the best."

I have till October 31 to show License to the Judge.

So I wasn't worried while I was up in middle of night with TV on, it was just too chilly to fall asleep again. Finally I got out a big down quilt, and instantly I was warm and cozy and fell asleep.

I was in the middle of a dream telling the head lifeguard of the public pool (Samantha) how women's liberation started.

"It was started by Shulie" I said. And I told her the story how Shulie started it in Chicago.

I was telling every detail of what happened there (I learned it all from Jo Freeman who was with her) when I looked up and in my dream there was Jo herself.

I said to Samantha "Here is Jo!" And I brought Samantha over to Jo.

Just when I arrived at Jo Freeman with Samantha and was going to go on with the story, the telephone woke me up.

It was Jim calling. It was quarter to 8.

I guess he overslept too. He said "I'll be there in 15 minutes."

Luckily during the two hours I was awake in the middle of the night, I had organized everything for going to the DMV.

LOL it was all stuff in 5 purses, plus I had my swim bag so we could swim afterwards no matter how it went.

Jim and I were both sleep befogged when he arrived. I forgot to put on my seatbelt for my warm up drive. I had been practicing wearing seatbelt for past two days so I would be used to it for test.

I pulled out of my driveway and drove the first easy

mile, then we switched seats.

I did one tushy turn in parking lot of bank where we switched seats to ask him if that is how he wants me to do it. He said yes.

He drove to DMV. I had to have my picture taken again and then we waited an hour.

He said "I wish they sold coffee and donuts here." He was dying for coffee.

But I had mine when I was up in middle of night.

Also 6 chocolate oreos.

I really wanted a cigarette while I was sitting at DMV but was afraid it would drain me.

This time I had a man examiner, I was glad, I am more relaxed with men.

The person ahead of me got the woman examiner.

The examiner and I waited for her to do her tushy turn. I guess she did it perfectly. I was praying for her. And then they drove off for the driving part.

He told me what to do, but I did not have to concentrate very hard because I had practiced it so much.

This time all the cones were in place, they never are when I practice on Sunday.

He said "If you think you are going to hit a cone, stop

and do it again. You get 3 tries.

"But if you do hit a cone you are disqualified."

When I did it, he said "You have to go back further to park it."

So I went back a little further. I did not have a problem with it.

Then he told me where to drive to and stop. So I knew I had passed that part of the test.

Then he got in next to me. For love or money he could not get the seatbelt to go all around him and buckle it.

I said "what if we try taking the pillow off."

I have to have pillows because the seats are worn away from the Arizona sun to the black bars with just a drop of foam rubber showing.

But then he put back the nice Indian blanket that Jim had brought over for examiner to sit on.

He still could not get it around him. It made us get close while I tried to help him. Finally he realized it was stuck in the door and if he got it out of the door he would have more room.

I thought it would be the same drive Jim and I had practiced and practiced every Sunday. We had followed the examiner to see the route and I knew it by heart.

But to my shock he said "Turn right!" instead of "Turn left."

So I drove a long distance on a road I had never driven on.

"Turn right here" he said.

This was a big road I had never been on. I was driving slowly.

He said "the speed limit is 40."

Jim had always pestered me to drive the speed limit but I ignored him. I always drove whichever speed was comfortable for me.

But because of that, I knew the examiner wanted me to step on it.

So I stepped on it and drove faster than I wanted to on a road I had never been on.

"Turn right at the light" he said.

I hoped the light would be red so I could organize myself.

But it kept staying green.

He said "It's green you have to go!"

I forgot to do my turn signal because I was focusing on making that turn at my big speed, and now light turned orange while I was doing it.

Then he told me which little road to turn into to go back to DMV.

Now I could switch to second. As soon as we got to DMV I switched to first. He told me to pull into a parking spot. I did.

He said "Now I will do the paper work, come inside and they will call your name."

It was far away from where Jim was waiting, watching everyone else do their tushy turn for the test. He was still talking to the man behind me, who was going to take his test after me.

The man had reassured me and Jim the route I would take was the same one we had practiced.

Right away I said "It was a whole different route." And I described it in case they made him drive that route too.

Then I went inside to wait for my name to be called.

I talked to the lady behind me. She showed me her wedding ring. It was a diamond and very pretty.

I just have the thin gold band which was my grandmother's.

Bill never got me a wedding ring.

I said "The examiner would not meet my eye when I went to the desk, is that a bad sign?"

She said "I am crossing my fingers for you."

I said how it took me 2 and a half years, altho when Jim started to teach me, he said "learning how to drive is easy, I can teach you in 5 minutes."

We chatted about her wedding ring. They called the numbers very loudly but you could barely hear it when they called out a name.

She said "I think that is your name." I had spaced out and forgot I was waiting to hear my name called.

When I went up she handed me what looked like my learners permit, but I guess it was my license. Because she said "it's done."

"You mean I passed," I said.

I jumped for joy.

"I could kiss you" I said.

I thought "they can't take away my license now," so since I had a few copies of *Pulled Over By The Cops* in my purse I gave one to her and one for her to give to the man examiner.

She was happy to get my book.

I thanked her and the man examiner very much and went outside to find Jim.

We trudged the long distance back to the truck where I

had parked it. Jim was overjoyed and excited beyond belief.

I couldn't find the car key. I took everything out of all 3 purses and emptied it into the straw bag I was carrying.

We retraced all our steps.

I saw the lady with the wedding ring, she said "ask at information." So I did.

Also I asked where I got my license. I said to Jim "they won't take away my license now that they see I am a fool and lost the car key?"

"No" he said.

But they didn't see my car key.

I had no energy left and no mind left so I could not even panic.

I tried looking in all my purses and in the straw bag, and by a miracle I found it.

It had been on the key ring my sister-in-law, Bill's sister, sent me 20 year ago as a Christmas present. She had no idea I did not know how to drive.

It was two very pretty pink enamel ballet slippers.

But it broke early this morning when I was first getting into the truck.

So when we were leaving DMV I said to Jim "drive me to Ace so I can buy a new key ring."

The Ace he took me to was a mile long.

I had to walk forever to find aisle 27 where key rings were.

I could not make up my mind.

I had no mind left. I grabbed two ice cold sodas, a tootsie pop for Jim, he likes that.

And walked the mile back to register in front of where Jim had parked.

How I succeeded in paying I have no idea. There was no mind.

I handed him his soda and tootsie pop but before he began to open it and drink it, he got call on his cellphone.

He had completely forgotten it was Tuesday and he was supposed to pick up his nephew to drive him to his job as cashier at movie theater.

It worked out perfectly because I had no mental energy to go to Y for my swim.

So he dropped me off at my house and we switched cars.

And I came in to write this as an email to my friends.

But instant I finished writing it and was going to fix the typos, my mind collapsed totally. I went in to watch 2 episodes of *Hazel*.

And my mind did not come back for 4 days. It took a week before I had the energy to fix the typos.

I thank all of you (my friends on email and everyone in Tucson) for all your encouragement and support. I never could have done it without you.

I love you.

Annie

I did it!

It was always Jim's dream for me that I be the girl
behind the wheel

He would have had an easier time teaching me to drive if
I had not been the driving student from hell

October 31

John, the Wonderful Cable Guy

My life has changed since I moved into Bill's tool room to be close to the heat. On Tuesday evening Frank was here all evening trying to set up the cable box on the old TV he gave me, but cable box turned out to be defective.

So the next afternoon, Wednesday afternoon, the cable man (John) arrived to do the job. LOL he was here all afternoon cause it turned out there was more involved than just setting up a new cable box.

Frank had run the cable wire into that room last year but John had to go up on the roof and redo Frank's work. Then he went into my backyard and redid the sagging telephone wires.

Then he went into my back bedroom and set up a new

remote for me for that cable tv cause I told him I had been having trouble with the old cable remote doing what I wanted it to do. I would press the buttons but they wouldn't change channels, they wouldn't mute.

He was here for 2 hours making everything ship shape for me. What an angel! It is his area of expertise so he did it all so fast and effortlessly compared to Frank.

I had planned to try to hang up my clothes all over the floor of the tool room carpet (LOL the only room in my house which still has carpet) .

There had been carpet in most of the rooms when we first moved in. But so many litters of kittens had been born who all used the carpeted rooms as their nursery until they were old enuf to want to go to the yard outside. Bill had to take up all the carpet and throw it in the garbage.

Even tho Cupcake's kittens were actually born in the tool room, they all rushed right in as soon as they could walk to join Priscilla's newest litter born in my computer room, so the tool room carpet is the only carpet which survived.

My clothes are all in a heap on the tool room floor altho I tried to kick them out of the way when I realized I hadn't picked them up in time for the cable guy, John.

John is such a sweetheart. I asked him if he hangs up his

clothes, and he says he is very fussy about his clothes. Apparently he takes perfect care of his clothes all the time. But he said he doesn't judge anyone who doesn't.

I said "I love clothes, I love pretty clothes, I love buying them but I don't take care of them at all. I just leave them on the floor. But I give a lot of care to my writing. When I publish a book I put a great deal of care into it."

I had planned when John left to give him my little women's lib book and also *Pulled Over By The Cops*.

I notice almost no one seems to want any of my novels when I offer them to them as gifts, but they are willing to accept my two little book, the women's lib one and *Pulled Over By the Cops*.

But even with them I have learned to ask "do you like to read?" before I offer them to them. Because when they say "no" they won't even accept my two little ones.

So you can imagine why I nearly went thru the roof with joy when John was leaving, and it turned out he not only wanted the two little ones but all my novels too.

Love Annie

A November to Remember

I can't believe all the things which go wrong in my life

8 am Thanksgiving morning, November 28th

From my Higher Self

I can't let Anne say adios without thanking Manuel for saving her truck.

An old lady going much faster than she should have been plowed into Anne's truck when her friend Doug had just fixed the minor start-up problem and was bringing it back to her.

The old lady's insurance found so many ways to get out of paying the big bucks to restore her truck. Said it had to be junked and gave her several hundred dollars.

Anne would have no truck at all, and not even enuf money to pay the insurance hike her own insurance was claiming because of the accident

When a great great angel come in to save Anne and her beloved truck.

Frank's brother-in-law Manuel came to look at it. He said it is very bad but he is able to do it.

He lowered his price so drastically when he found insurance is giving her bupkis, that Anne was able to afford paying Manuel to fix up her truck.

He said when he brings it back to her it will be "like new."

On behalf of Heaven and of Anne, We thank Manuel with all our heart.

This was the morning before Thanksgiving, so Anne knew she would have a nice Thanksgiving after all.

I am going to give the last word to Harry, the wonderful husband of Anne's friend Jan.

The evening before Thanksgiving Anne emailed Jan the whole story of what happened.

Anne woke up on Thanksgiving morning to this email from Harry

From: Harry
To: Anne
Sent: Thursday, November 28, 2013 12:20 AM
Subject: Re: Insurance did not come thru, but thank God for Manuel

Good for you, Anne. So happy things turned out well! There are angels in our midst, sweet human angels of kindness and love. -- Harry

It began with a phone call

On the afternoon of November 13th I was happily posting on FaceBook when Jim called.

"How are you?" he said

"Great" I said.

"Well you won't be anymore."

"Why?" I said.

"Call Doug" he said

"You tell me. What happened?"

"He was bringing your truck back to you when someone crashed into it."

I called Doug.

"We are waiting for the Sheriff.

"You will faint when you see your truck."

Luckily he had prepared me for the sight of it.

When the tow truck delivered it to my front yard it was totally mangled.

Manuel To The Rescue

I became desperate when car insurance did not come thru

Anne is in bliss. The great angel Manuel saved her truck for her

I email my friend Robert Roth back in NYC

From: Annie
To: Robert
Sent: Sunday, December 01, 2013 8:37 AM
Subject: Happy 4th day of Chanukah

Hi Robert

Happy 4th day of Chanukah or is it the 5th.

In any case Chanukah is very special to me this year because on Thanksgiving (also the first day of Chanukah this year) Manuel and his two helpers arrived to drive my truck to his shop (i.e. his backyard) so its monumental booboos can be fixed.

Truck is with Dr Manuel as we speak

Love, Annie

From: Robert
To: Annie
Sent: Sunday, December 01, 2013 8:45 AM
Subject: Re: Happy 4th day of Chanukah

Thanks. And give Manuel a big hello from his New York fan club.

December 16th

Truck is back and better than new

Anne jumps for joy when she sees her truck

I instantly email all my friends

From: Annie
Sent: Monday, December 16, 2013 5:52 PM
Subject: Great news! Truck is back and better than new

Manuel just brought the truck back to me. It looks better than new. He even put in a new seat for me. The old seat was destroyed by the sun. The upholstery was gone.

And the mountain of work he had to do to make my totally mangled truck better than new is mind boggling.

He is the greatest angel of the universe. And to do it for me for such tiny money is a colossal favor.

This is the greatest Christmas present in the world.

I am ecstatic that Manuel did that for me.

Love, Anne

The first one to email me back was Jo Freeman

From: Jo
To: Annie
Sent: Monday, December 16, 2013 6:10 PM

Bake him some cookies to show your appreciation.

So that evening when I emailed my friend Robert Roth back in my old neighborhood in NYC I told him my great news, plus Jo's idea I bake cookies for Manuel.

From: Robert
To: Annie
Sent: Tuesday, December 17, 2013 5:37 AM
Subject: Re: Great news! Truck is back and better than new

What a fantastic turn of events. First Manuel, absolutely fantastic. His New York fan club is beyond thrilled.

Then Jo. Met her during Shulie's memorial. Knew she had great ideas. Wanted to say this one takes the cake. But thought better of it. But decided to anyway.

One day will ride in truck with you and eat some cookies.

love,

Robert

December 18

The 'hood

Yesterday morning was huge.

I was up nearly the whole night before it, thinking about it, preparing for it, even trying not to fret about it.

Jo Freeman had emailed me the evening before suggesting I bake cookies for Manuel to show my appreciation for what he did for me.

But I have not done any baking since I was in junior high school. Marsha Appelbaum and I used to bake chocolate chip cookies and brownies when I was over at her house after school.

Marsha went on baking. We just got on email together, and her emails tell me the wonderful dinners she cooked and the wonderful things she baked for dessert for dinner guests in Florida.

But except for baking corn bread for my boyfriend Alan during a snowstorm when we lived together when we were both at City College, I have never baked a single thing after all those chocolate chip cookies with Marsha.

Chocolate chip cookies are not hard to make, the recipe is right on the back of the bag of chocolate chips.

I seem to remember you need white sugar and brown sugar. I don't remember what else. And cookie tin that you put butter on so the cookies slide off.

Maybe butter in the cookies too?

What about flour?

And a working oven of course.

Our mothers had all these things, so it was easy for us.

All I have is sugar, it would be an enterprise for me.

But I loved Jo's idea of bringing Manuel delicious cookies as thank you present.

So I decided as soon as I woke up the next morning I would have Jim drive me to the Jewish bakery.

And buy their beautiful assortment of little cookies as Manuel's present.

I never buy them for myself, the price is steep, but they are the most delicious cookies in the world, other than the ones you bake for yourself.

Their cookies are out of the world delish.

Also I discovered in the evening before I went to bed that I have to bring the truck to DMV for vehicle inspection before I am allowed to drive it.

So I planned to do that after going to Nadine's kosher bakery for Manuel's cookies.

And then because I was up all night thinking about everything I was going to do the next morning and how I would do it.

I decided I would also bring Manuel a copy of each one of my books, my 5 novels and my little womens lib book and *Pulled Over By The Cops*.

I'd given them all to Frank way back, I didn't know then that Frank does not read.

So it had not occurred to me to give them to Manuel.

Who gives books to people who do not read!

I hadn't thought of my books as just as an ornament before. I don't think Manuel, Frank's brother-in-law, likes to read either, but I thought he might like them as an ornament.

Altho god forbid I add clutter to anyone's house

I had given Manuel *Pulled Over By the Cops* when he brought me back the truck. I thought he would like the cartoons in it. Which he does!

But I decided when I was up all night that I would bring him all my books, he might like them as a possession.

Giggle giggle they may wind up being the only books in Manuel's house.

He has the complete library of Anne Wilensky's novels, plus her little womens lib book.

Which Helen, Pat, Peggy and Shulie are in. Giggle giggle they will all wind up in Manuel's house.

Which I discovered is the equivalent of the Lower East Side of New York.

It is our old neighborhood. And altho Manuel is such a good boy and just does body work in his yard Jim told me that it is not only good boys like Manuel who live there, because it is where everyone goes to buy pot, *etc.*

I had never been in that neighborhood till Jim took me there after DMV to bring the kosher cookies to Manuel. And I giggled my head off that I had found the neighborhood where everyone goes to buy pot, *etc.*

"You're in the hood" Jim kept saying to me.

It's handy for me to know that because now when I try to tell Jim where Bill and I lived in NYC I can say we lived in the hood and Jim will know what it means.

He knows the Tucson hood very well so he could extrapolate what the NYC hood is.

I had no idea Tucson even had a hood.

Probably if Bill and I knew Tucson had a hood we would have moved there when we left NYC. Because we were so used to living in a hood and were so comfortable there.

But instead I had called my aunt in Tucson and said "Rent us an apt. which accepts dogs."

And of course she rented us an apartment in the neighborhood where aunts live.

It is the neighborhood where all her friends live.

Bill and I fainted when we first arrived. It was so absolutely different from where we had been living.

We would have been so comfortable in the sweet little hood Jim took me to yesterday.

I would have felt so at home next to Manuel the Mexican body worker.

He is just like all my neighbors in NYC except he is Mexican, they are Italian.

Carmine my neighbor did not read or write either, just like Frank.

I am used to that.

Frank is tall and good looking but Carmine looked exactly like Manuel when he was the same age as Manuel.

Short and stocky and so warm.

LOL it took me 22 years to find my Carmine LoCicero in Tucson.

He turns out to be a body worker who lives in the hood.

Carmine was born in the hood in NYC and lived there his whole life

And the same with Manuel.

Altho I think Frank and his 13 brothers and sisters grew up in South Tucson.

But one of his sisters married Manuel and now lives with Manuel in the hood.

I recognized Manuel's house because Frank said he decorated his sister's yard for Christmas.

It is the same way he decorated his own yard a few doors down from me.

And the same way he decorated my yard.

When Frank offered to decorate my yard for Christmas the first Christmas that Bill was in Heaven, this was 2 years ago.

I said "yes, thank you."

But in fact it was a shock to me when I saw it when he

finished.

It wouldn't have been shocking if it was someone else's yard.

But in my whole life I never expected to have a front yard with a huge cross and in huge letters across it Happy Birthday Jesus.

I had actually thought it was sweet and wonderful when I had first seen it in Frank's yard when he rented the house across the street.

But after the trauma my mother went thru when she was a little girl in Rochester.

And her door was the only one which did not have a wreath on it for Christmas.

And the children in her class taunted her about it.

And she begged her mother and her mother said no.

When I visited her in her fancy apt. complex in Walnut Creek CA when she first moved there.

And I saw the wreaths up on everyone's apartment door I wanted to say

"You're a big girl now Mom, you can have your heart's desire and put up a wreath on your door too."

The last Christmas Bill was here, he did decorate for Christmas, he got a lovely wreath for our front door.

And put up white fairy lights all over the huge cactus in our front yard.

It was so beautiful I cried with joy.

But none of that prepared me for what Frank did in my yard the following Christmas.

A huge cross with the huge banner across it Happy Birthday Jesus.

And that was just the start of it.

LOL he made my yard look like all the other yards in the hood.

When I wanted to tell someone here in Tucson that I am shocked that is my own front yard.

That Jewish girls from New York City do not have a front yard that looks like that.

There was no one I could tell who would understand.

I said to Jim, "look what Frank did!"

He said "very nice."

But the next year when Frank offered to do the same thing, I said "I think I will just have the fairy lights all over the huge cactus and the wreath and that is fine."

It was such a relief to me that it looked just like what Billy had done.

But this Christmas when Frank arrived with his son, and

said "do you want the white lights or the color lights on your big cactus," I could not resist all the pretty colors.

And he jazzed up the wreath too, put a little snowman in there, and added pine cones, colored lights.

I love it.

He gave me very pretty Christmas decorations this year, I am very happy.

So naturally I recognized Manuel's house instantly.

It is a tiny yard, like all the yards in the hood.

Not a huge giant yard like the yards in my neighborhood.

But sure enuf there is the big cross with Happy Birthday Jesus in banner across it.

I guess Frank has decorated for his sister again.

O what a trip.

I guess you can take the girl out of the hood but you can't take the hood out of the girl.

I felt so at home in that neighborhood.

Everything about it looked and felt so familiar to me.

It is where I belong.

But of course if I lived there I would not have Frank on one side of me and Jim on the other side.

And would not have my new life OUT OF THE HOOD.

And I love my new life too.

I love my huge backyard where all the birds come.

And a wonderful hawk did arrive in the big tree in the middle of my yard two days ago.

And looked at me standing on my patio and I looked at him.

And we each both stood there for quite a while.

Then I wanted to go back to putting my dishes in the dishwasher and he wanted to fly off.

Now I am a girl who has dishwasher and hawk who visits me in my backyard.

It is good to have new life too.

Altho my heart will always be in the hood.

Gracias Manuel

Manuel is the best bodyworker of all time. I couldn't believe my eyes when I walked out my front door and saw my truck looking like it had just arrived from the factory.

I danced around my yard in joy. And I could not stop kissing him.

Jo said "bake him cookies to show your appreciation." But how can you ever show your appreciation to an angel. Because your appreciation is bottomless.

"How did you ever do it?" I asked him

"It was a lot of work," he said.

God bless you my darling, you saved a girl in deep distress.

And thereby saved everyone. Doug felt horrible when he had to return the truck to me that way.

Jim dreaded making that phone call telling me what happened to my truck

You turned a catastrophe into a joy for all.

I love you

Annie

Afterword

January 14, 2014

*Sebastian, my wonderful lifeguard, takes pic of truck in the
Y parking lot so I can send it to my friends on email*

*LOL that is Jim's shoulder in corner of pic
And our mountains to the north*

February 14, 2014

*After our swim Jim and I get into my pretty white truck
and drive to Mi Nidito for my celebration lunch for getting
my Drivers License*

February 14, 2014

Lunch at Mi Nidito

Two years ago Jim had promised "I will take you out to lunch when you get your Drivers License."

I think I had been learning how to drive for 6 months then. Neither of us knew then it would be a forever time till I actually did get my license. I think we anticipated 6 more months, a year from when I got my Learners Permit.

But it was a forever time, which is not completely my fault. Life had its way with me too. But the result is I had 2 years to discuss happily in the car what restaurant I wanted to be taken to for my celebration lunch.

Jim and I never go to a restaurant and I haven't been to a restaurant in ages. After the pool we stop for some fast food take-out which each of us eats in front of our own tv when we get back to our own home.

It really was huge deal for me that I was going to be taken to a restaurant and treated. I kept changing in my mind which restaurant I wanted to go to. Giggle giggle I knew this was something which would happen only once.

At some point it got changed to breakfast. I said "After I pass my test I want you to take me and Alice out for breakfast at Village Inn, I can order their crepes suzettes."

I didn't stick with this plan in my mind, but I must have told Alice this at the time. "When I get my license Jim is taking both of us out for breakfast."

I never bothered to tell her I had changed to lunch in a restaurant. But it was at this point that it became Jim would treat me and Alice for lunch.

Finally the summer before I got my license I settled in my own mind which restaurant I wanted. Mi Nidito because I kept hearing about it from others. This is a Mexican restaurant in South Tucson which has been here forever.

After that I began happily kibitzing in the car with Jim about what I was going to order.

"Bring your wallet, bring two credit cards, this is not going to be cheap" I would say. "I never order iced tea with my Mexican meal even tho I always want it, because I want to save money, I just drink water. But I am going to have iced tea.

"And I am going to have dessert too. I will get fried ice cream. And Alice likes to drink, you can treat her to a margarita. She loves that. Treat her to two margaritas."

"What are you going to order?" I asked.

"A taco and enchilada" he said.

"That is what you always get at take out fast food. I guess it is better there tho."

"A lot better" he said.

"Is it expensive there?"

He said "no."

"O just like any Mexican restaurant?" I asked.

"Yes" he said.

Finally the plan was we'd go on Valentines Day. I hear about margaritas all the time, they sound delicious but I don't like the effect of alcohol on me, my mind blurs.

I asked the teen age lifeguard on Monday if I can have one at Mi Nidito without alcohol. He said "yes ask for a virgin margarita."

So I planned to do that. Jim simply tuned me out when I went on and on about my virgin margarita.

I discovered when he is driving, he doesn't listen to a word I say, because he is totally involved in looking at the girl in the car next to us.

For Jim driving does not need he has to pay attention the way it is with me. So he spends his whole time noticing the beautiful girl in the next car and wishing he could have her as his girlfriend.

He could care less about me elaborating what I am going to order at Mi Nidito. We live in two different worlds. I am lost in the glory of my lunch, he just cares about beautiful wimin.

The day before yesterday we worked out the plan about going. He said "The parking lot is always very full, there is a long wait there to get inside. So I'll take you swimming late, that way we will miss the lunch crowd and get to park in the parking lot.

"We'll arrive at 1:30."

"Perfect!" I said, "you call Alice and tell her to meet us there then."

There was a parking space. Jim drove, it is way too hard a drive for the level I am at now.

Alice was already there and it is a big treat for me to see her. I only see her about once a year. But she belongs to same club as Jim, they see each other in the steam room nearly every day. And plus she calls him on the phone nearly every day. They are best friends.

It makes for an incredibly relaxing 3 some that Jim and Alice have been best friends before I met either one of them. And Jim is best friends with both of us. And Alice and I are good friends. Each of us is totally relaxed with the other and with both others.

We drove thru the most run down part of Tucson to get there. It was hard for me to believe this restaurant I heard so much about could be in the middle of this totally run down area.

It was almost all families coming in when we arrived. Both Mexican and American. With kids and teenage daughters. A lot of couples too, but either our age, or few years younger. A Friday afternoon everyone is back at work.

Jim went inside and told them we are waiting. That's the way it works. When you arrive you tell them you are waiting, and then they call your name when a table is cleared for you.

So me and Jim and Alice sat outside and smoked. Jim smoked his cigar, I offered Alice my cigs. We sat outside with all the other people who were waiting to be called for their table. I guess everyone there had been here before and settled down happily and comfortably for the long wait.

And I told the lady next to me that Alice is an artist. Alice had one of those post cards galleries give you of her painting of "The Dove and Hawk" and she showed it to the lady. Who showed it to her husband.

The lady was in love with it. "It is a beauty." And she was so happy when Alice said "you can keep it" when she was going to give it back.

It was really very pleasant sitting outside in the warm sunshine smoking cigs. The nice lady was sitting next to me. Alice and Jim were across from us, her husband was across too. It was a low wall, very comfortable to sit on. I guess there were about 40 people up there, everyone happy and relaxed in the sunshine. LOL some of the little children were lying down on that broad short wall.

It is definitely a family affair and no one was dressed up at all. Altho Alice was wearing very nice Mexican dress and all her beautiful Mexican jewelry.

And I had dressed for going to a restaurant. On Valentines Day. A short red skirt, a bra, and fuchsia top. LOL I looked like a valentine. Jim wore his same shorts and tee shirt he always wears.

Everyone seemed to be wearing what they happened to be wearing. I was the only one who wore a special outfit. LOL but for me it was big occasion.

As soon as we sat down I said "Have a margarita Alice." She was so surprised and overjoyed. There really is something so nice about socializing with zero strain at all. I don't think I've had that since I was a kid.

Alice did most of the talking, but because there were two of us, Jim and I could each tune into the parts of her conversation which interested us.

And when we got in the truck to leave Jim commented "Alice is a knowledgeable woman." Which is high praise for Jim, I never heard him praise anyone.

Alice did live for 20 years in the mountains of Mexico, and I found that part of her conversation very interesting.

I ordered horchata, a Mexican rice drink with my meal, delicious. And when it was time for dessert, I ordered flan. They don't serve fried ice cream there.

And I said to Alice "would you like dessert or second margarita or both?"

She didn't want dessert she wanted a second margarita. Her eyes lit up but she looked at Jim. She didn't know if he could afford it. But I knew that Jim's social security check and pension check had begun arriving this month. The long wait of never having enuf money is over. He is in the money now.

I guess he hasn't told Alice, she really wanted that second margarita but was afraid to accept at first because of Jim's pocketbook.

"Go ahead!" I said to Alice, "do you want dessert too?" She said "no."

But boy was that girl happy about getting her second margarita. When the first one arrived she said "it is not strong". But apparently they make a mango margarita which is out of this world. She loved sipping on the first one.

I had noticed it had taken her a long time to finish drinking her first one. The 10 minute wait while we took such a long time deciding what we each wanted to order. Then ten minutes while waiting for the food to arrive. And she was half way thru her meal when she finally finished it.

The food was scrumptious but more than I am used to eating at one time now. So while we were waiting for Alice's second margarita to arrive, I put all the food I had not been able to finish in the two boxes the wonderful waitress brought us.

I never saw such an efficient operation as the way they operated that restaurant.

It is all done so superbly. So many people at so many tables, yet everything done so perfectly.

I liked our waitress very much, altho she had no extra time for chit chat. But when I said "Gracias senorita," she called me senorita too, which made me giggle out loud with delight. It was so much fun being called senorita.

No one ever has before.

LOL when Alice's margarita arrived I knew it was going to be another twenty minutes while she sipped on it. I asked if we could take it out to the wall so I could smoke cigarette while she sipped, and Jim could have his cigar. But they said we are not allowed to take alcohol outside.

So as soon as Ana, our waitress brought the check, it was $43 which I thought was a bargain for all that. I put 12 dollars down on the table for a tip. And I told them I was going outside to smoke cigs.

Alice had brought both me and Jim a present, a tiny baby cactus, with a beautiful small rock, and lovely seashell, in a beautiful hand made ceramic pot.

So I took mine and my take-out food and put it in the

back of the truck. And then sat happily on the wall in sunshine smoking cigs and watching all the families arrive.

The teenage girls with their parents. And the little ones with their parents too. Everyone looked so happy. You remember as a kid how much fun it was when your parents took the family out to a restaurant.

It didn't take as long as I thought it would for her to sip her second margarita. Because I looked up and there was Jim.

He said "Alice is in the bathroom."

And when I looked up again there was both of them.

Jim had instantly lit up his cigar, and he did not look one bit frustrated that he had to sit there while Alice sipped her second margarita. I was surprised because I knew he was ready to go when I was.

But he looked totally happy and content.

And Alice was swimming in bliss. She loved her lunch and outing with us.

And when I got home I saw that I was pleased as punch too. "It's all about making Alice happy" I realized. For me anyway.

I don't know why Jim was so happy, I guess he liked making both of us happy.

Altho he did remark half to himself, "well that's out of the way now. Good."

And he did drive as fast as he could and try to make every light, because he really wanted to get home now. Feed the dogs and relax in front of his TV.

For a girl who never goes out at all, just drive to pool with Jim beside me, drive to grocery store with Jim beside me, stop for take-out tacos with Jim beside me, and drive home

It was all a major outing.

But as I said to Jim when I ordered the second margarita for Alice and dessert for me, on his wallet, "this is an occasion which will never happen again."

Alice was so cute. I don't remember whether it was before we went inside and were all smoking and chatting in the sunshine, or when we were standing around afterward for a smoke together.

She said "I don't know why I got invited, I didn't do anything," she meant contributing to me getting my license.

She said "I thought we were going to go out for waffles for breakfast."

I forgot that Alice still thought that was the plan.

The instant I emailed her "I got my License this

morning."

She emailed back "breakfast."

I have no idea why making Alice happy is the joy of my life, but that seems to be the size of it.

The End

So my darling readers

Till next time.

I wish you all blue skies and bright sunshine and let

everything come up roses for you.

I love you

Annie

Tucson Arizona
April 13th 2014

An open letter to anyone who wants to write or even dreams of doing it

Go for it!
Writing is easy and fun
Here is my experience

November is National Write a Novel in a Month and a month before November '08, my friend Lisa in Tucson told me about it, and suggested I do it. But I was used to writing short stories and posting them on my Blog (the stories are mostly about my yesterday)— I never wrote a novel and didn't know how.

So I just wrote polite thank you back to Lisa.

But thank God she pushed me. Because when November 3rd rolled around, I decided to give it a try. And to my big surprise, I loved doing it.

I just went to my machine when I woke up with cup of coffee and pack of cigarettes, and wrote for 45 minutes each morning for 3 straight weeks. I still spent my afternoons and evenings posting on current events forum.

I was doing it for a week when Lisa encouraged me to register at the site (NANO) (it is free) and then I received their pep-talk emails, which they sent out to everyone.

Lisa was doing it too, even tho she had never written in her life, she is a painter.

But this is a great way for anyone who has ever dreamed of being a writer to do it. Every November there is another one. I hope you consider doing it too. All you have to do is write for 45 minutes each day for month of November. No editing! No re-writing!

You can begin by telling about your yesterday too, but after you have done that several times, start to write a story which is long enough to hold your interest to keep telling it for a while.

(Telling a story means "and then" "and then" "and then." First this happened, then that happened, then that happened, then that happened.)

This will give you experience in narrative (telling a story) and there is very good chance that in the middle you will "find your own voice."

This means right in the middle of telling your story, suddenly you hear a voice in your head dictating a different story.

This one is about your earliest childhood, it is all things you have forgotten, and the voice is different, it is in the first person (even if you have been writing in 3rd person) and it is very personal. And you will love it!

If this happens, immediately stop writing what you were writing, and instead start writing everything you are hearing.

This is called "finding your own voice" as a writer, it makes writing so easy and fun, you just take down what it says— or as they say "you get out of the way, and the story writes itself."

That is the way I became a writer back in NYC. I was in my late 20s then and had just been fired from my job. Bill was working as Wall Street messenger then for $96/week. He said "why don't you become a writer, I will support you." I thought it was a great idea, I decided to do it.

So I wrote three tiny 2 page stories about my yesterday and then sat down to write long story, I wrote it in 3rd person and it was about a love affair before I met my husband. That topic interested me enough to keep telling the story.

But right in the middle of it, I was a few weeks into it, I heard that voice dictating a whole other story. It was my littlest little girl experiences.

It is the same as learning how to balance on a bicycle. One day they are supporting you, and you are pedaling, and then suddenly out of nowhere, you balance. You can ride a bike.

You never thought it would happen to you, even tho you watched all your friends do it, because it looks like magic.

It is the same way with writing. You push yourself along telling a story, and then suddenly you balance. You hear that voice and simply take down what it says. The story writes itself, you get out of the way.

But you can only learn how to balance on a bike when you are on a bike, and you can only hear your own voice, while you are at the machine writing. But it is as natural and effortless as learning how to balance on a bike. It comes to all.

Guess what! CreateSpace owned by Amazon publishes any book written by anyone for free, but you have to do all the work yourself. No one even reads it.

You have to format it for a paperback book, all they do is press a button to print and bind it, and post it for sale on Amazon.

When I saw the technical work involved in formatting my novel into a paperback book I was terrified. I didn't even know what they were talking about or how to do any of it.

But I was too deep into it to quit. I wanted to publish my novel now, I didn't just want it lost on my computer.

It turns out CreateSpace has community boards. And there are angels on it (people who have published lots and lots of books, are completely experienced) and they walk us newbies thru everything. Ones even less experienced than me, they wrote their book and don't even know how to indent a paragraph or what a tab is or how to edit.

It turned out everything which seemed impossibly hard when I first heard about it, is not hard, you just press a button in your word processing program.

But of course I needed to learn from the community boards which button? where? things like that. They have the patience of saints there and love to help.

I tell you all this because it is God's gift to writers. That we can publish ourselves.

CreateSpace also does videos, and music, photography books, art books, comic books.

Lulu does this too. It was first started by Lulu.com. Everyone at CreateSpace started there. Both places are wonderful and many publish at both places. Both Lulu and CreateSpace are free, they publish your book for free and post it on Amazon. A gift from Heaven to all artists.

I tell you all this to encourage you to go for it! If I could do it anyone can. Before I began writing I was convinced I didn't have a creative bone in my body.

I had always loved writing book reports and compositions for school, and always loved writing letters. But I was never artistic in anyway.

Because it turns out it is all there under the surface for everyone. But you have to be willing to give it a whirl for it to emerge. There is no such thing as talent. It is only when you are actually doing it, that interesting and surprising things happen.

Writing is a big treat you give yourself, because it is way to get to know yourself.

It is never too late to start. Whenever you do is the perfect time. And there is nothing to compare with the freshness of your early beginning.

So think of starting writing, as like the beginning of Spring. Later you will develop more skills, but there is nothing like the beginning. When all the miracles, freshness and inspiration happen.

I wish you luck on your enterprise!

I love you, Anne

Haiku Helen Press

Novels by Anne Wilensky

Ruthie Has a New Love

Girl Blog From Tucson

MORE Girl Blog From Tucson

Sweet Sound of Bird Song

Haboob

My little womens lib book is:

Not What You'd Expect
How the womens liberation movement started
My personal experience of it

Pulled Over By The Cops is from *Topsy Turvy*, the 4
chapters about going to court, etc.

Haiku Helen Press is Anne Pyne and Helen Kritzler who met in the womens liberation movement in the Sixties and have been friends ever since.

Annie and Helen are Haiku Helen Press

Cover designed by Helen Kritzler
Drawings on front cover and back cover by Helen
Kritzler

Drawing by Helen Kritzler

www.ingramcontent.com/pod-product-compliance
Lightning Source LLC
Chambersburg PA
CBHW071246170626
46809CB00001B/93